In the
St. Nick of Time

The Sullivan Boys, Book Five

by

K. M. Daughters

This is a work of fiction. Names, characters, places, and incidents are either the product of the author's imagination or are used fictitiously, and any resemblance to actual persons living or dead, business establishments, events, or locales, is entirely coincidental.

In the St. Nick of Time: The Sullivan Boys, Book Five

COPYRIGHT © 2011 by K. M. Daughters

Cover Art by *Nicola Martinez*

The Wild Rose Press
PO Box 706
Adams Basin, NY 14410-0706
Visit us at www.thewildrosepress.com

Publishing History
First Crimson Rose Edition, 2010
ISBN 1-60154-903-2

Published in the United States of America

"You must be Kay."

She jumped at the masculine voice.

"Your brothers have been waiting for you." The stranger leaned against a half-painted post, his face hidden in the shadows. "Need help with the cookies?"

"No, thanks." Kay admired the rippling muscles across his back as he bent to drop the paintbrush in the pan and turned, advancing toward her. His crystal green eyes twinkled, snug jeans rode low on slim hips. Bare-chested, he strode with athletic grace. V*ery nice.* She shivered, an unexpected, lustful surge zipping through her.

Adjusting the foil that covered the tray, Kay said, "How did you know I had cookies?"

"Every five minutes or so, one of your brothers yells, 'Where is Kay with the cookies?'" The laugh lines around his eyes deepened with his genuine smile.

"Nice to be wanted," she grumbled. Shifting the tray on her hip, she gripped the screen door's handle.

"Hey, I bet my sisters never looked at their watches and wondered, 'Where's Flynn with the Guinness and chips?'" His infectious smile crinkled the corners of his eyes. "My brothers-in-law, maybe, but definitely not my sisters."

Kudos for K. M. Daughters and...

AGAINST DOCTORS ORDERS
The Sullivan Boys, Book One
2009 The Lories, 3rd Place, Romantic Suspense
"An intriguing story, full of detailed scenes and fascinating, believable characters."
~WR Potter, Reader's Choice Reviews (5 Stars)
"This story has it all."
~Got Erotic Romance Reviews (4 Diamonds)

BEYOND THE CODE OF CONDUCT
The Sullivan Boys, Book Two
2010 Borders Books READERS CROWN FINALIST
2010 THE Lories, 2nd Place, Romantic Suspense
#6 Top Ten Books of 2009, The Book Connection
"This story is hot hot hot!"
~Val Pearson, You Gotta Read Book Reviews
"Plenty of big-Irish-family passion, lush descriptions and lots of emotion...from its exciting beginning to its unexpected ending."
~Between the Lines Book Reviews (Fantastic)

CAPTURING KARMA
The Sullivan Boys, Book Three
"The author writes with such a warm, flowing style, it's like visiting old friends."
~Cindy Himler, RT Book Reviews
"A fantastic read!"
~Night Owl Romance (Top Pick, 4.5 Stars)

ALL'S FAIR IN LOVE AND LAW
The Sullivan Boys, Book Four
"In one word, this book is Awesome!"
~The Book Connection

Dedication

For Joelle, our sister of the heart.
The Sullivan Boys stories end, but
our friendship continues...

Prologue

*Blend in, act concerned, just one of the crowd.
"What happened? Is he all right? Someone call 911."*

*The fallen man—a heap of red velvet and white
fur topped with a merry Santa hat, littered the
sidewalk like a big bag of garbage. No, a big bag of
wind.*

*Too late for you, you stupid bastard. Ho, ho, ho.
You're the first to go.*

*Yes, Virginia, there is a Santa Claus...but not
for long.*

Chapter 1

Kay peered through the windshield at the ramshackle lake house and prepared to face her family, her white-knuckled hands curled around the steering wheel. Her brothers, although dear, had treated her like a porcelain statue, perilously breakable and lifeless, since Mike died. *They have to stop walking on eggshells around me.*

She didn't want their pity or their protection. Struggling to accept that her husband was gone forever had consumed Kay's every waking minute for nearly two years. But Mike Lynch was dead, and she had no choice but to accept the fact. The time had come for a decision. She could either wallow in despair or live again.

Kay chose life. *Time to scramble some eggs.* Filled with determination, she popped the hatch, swung her door open, and slid out of the oversized SUV. Ducking under the raised rear hatch, she strapped a work belt around her hips and tucked a painter's cap over her new hairdo. Jet-black spikes beneath the hat's brim were reflected in the car's mirror. *The new me.*

She had banished her natural blonde pixie cut at the salon. Maybe forever.

Leave it to her brothers to cloak rehabbing with the reinstated, annual Halloween party theme they had selected—Painters and Carpenters. Gazing at the house, she surveyed the weathered shingles, scraped bare of peeling paint in spots, and the new wood steps, heaped with sawdust, leading to a dilapidated porch. To her brothers' credit, the old summerhouse's condition had improved since she'd last seen it. She grinned. *It's almost habitable now.*

Biceps flexing, she hoisted the heavy tray of cookies out of the trunk. Balancing the tray on her hip, she managed to slam the hatch closed. A saw's grating whine and clopping hammers filled the damp, crisp air. Squaring her shoulders for battle, she squinted into the sun and glided up the yet unpainted wooden steps.

"You must be Kay." She jumped at the masculine voice.

"Your brothers have been waiting for you." The stranger leaned against a half-painted post, his face hidden in the shadows. "Need help with the cookies?"

"No, thanks." Kay admired the rippling muscles across his back as he bent to drop the paintbrush in the pan and turned, advancing toward her. His crystal green eyes twinkled and snug jeans rode low on slim hips. Bare-chested, he strode with athletic grace. V*ery nice.* She shivered, an unexpected, lustful surge zipping through her.

Adjusting the foil that covered the tray, Kay said, "How did you know I had cookies?"

"Every five minutes or so, one of your brothers yells, 'Where is Kay with the cookies?'" The laugh lines around his eyes deepened with his genuine smile.

"Nice to be wanted," she grumbled. Shifting the tray on her hip, she gripped the screen door's handle.

"Hey, I bet my sisters never looked at their watches and wondered, 'Where's Flynn with the Guinness and chips?'" His infectious smile crinkled the corners of his eyes. "My brothers-in-law, maybe, but definitely not my sisters."

"Flynn? Your name sounds familiar."

"I work with your brother, Pat."

He swung his arm over her head, easing the screen door open. Her hand fell away from the handle, his musky scent pervading her senses. Swiveling, Flynn flattened his back against the screen, propping the door open, and faced her, relaxed, a warm smile lighting his green eyes.

"Pat's mentioned you. Flynn Dowd the wunderkind!"

Flynn shrugged, nonchalant.

"What has it been? Maybe a year, and your profiling helped close six cold cases already? Amazing." Kay exclaimed.

"Just doing my job."

"It will be exciting to work with you."

Flynn's brow furrowed. "Work?"

"Where's Kay with the cookies?" Joe bellowed from somewhere out back.

Flynn grinned. "Told you."

Disarming man. "You sure did. My brother Joe beckons." Kay chuckled. "Better get these to the locusts. Want one before they disappear?"

"Yes, I certainly do."

Flynn reached under the foil, withdrew a cookie dotted with melted chips, and popped it in his mouth.

Kay's eyes were drawn to his full lips as his captivating tongue licked a smear of dark chocolate from the corner of his mouth. Her nerve endings fired another sensual blast.

"Now I know why they've been so impatient for you to arrive." His eyes met hers, steady, penetrating, and a slow smile spread on those compelling lips. "These cookies are phenomenal."

Yeah, it's all about the baked goods with me. I'll show them. Kay proceeded through the open door, and Flynn snatched two more from under the foil as she passed him.

"Talk to you later," she called over her shoulder.

4

****

"Well, finally! Where have you been? You were supposed to be here an hour ago." Pat strode across the brownish grass, a barbecue lighter in his huge hand, and mounted the rickety stairs to the deck where Kay stood.

"Good to see you too, Pat," Kay retorted, standing on tiptoe to kiss her brother's cheek.

Another pair of Sullivan brothers left their workstations at the back of the house and descended on the tray Kay toted, like bees to honey. Kay held her ground against the jostling of multiple hand swipes as the cookie collection dwindled.

"Hey, save some for us." Bobbie demanded. Joe Sullivan's wife set a platter of hotdogs and hamburgers down on the makeshift table set up next to an ancient brick grill in the yard.

One by one, the Sullivan clan filed toward the tray of cookies. In a defensive maneuver, Kay slid the tray onto the flat-topped railing and cleared out of their way, balancing the tray with one hand as she observed her family.

Joe, his jaws chomping, drew Bobbie down into his lap in a beat-up Adirondack chair, laughing playfully as she squirmed to escape. Matty stood serenely next to Brian, her hand resting over their baby's barely visible bump on her abdomen.

Charlie DeMarco tilted her head toward her fiancé Pat's position back at the grill, giving Kay's hand a squeeze. "Kay, tell this big lug that a little charcoal fluid won't hurt anything. By the time he gets this fire started, it will be Thanksgiving."

"The fire is ready now," Pat called smugly.

Kay's older brother, Danny, stepped out onto the deck and waited for his wife Molly to follow him before he slid the glass door closed behind her. Sorrow pinched inside Kay, missing Mike amid the couples.

"Hey, Kay, you finally made it. How's Ma?" Danny asked, referring to Jean Sullivan. The quiet matriarch of the brood had voluntarily remained behind at Kay's house to shepherd her grandchildren.

Danny left Molly's side and hurried toward Kay, eyeing the sparse cookies remaining on the tray.

"You know Mom," Kay responded. "She has everything under control, as usual. She might even let Daddy help her."

The brothers ringed the grill, voicing conflicting advice about how to grill the perfect burger. Pat stoically swung the spatula, ignoring all the recommendations.

The women darted in and out of the house and climbed up and down the deck stairs bringing bowls of salads and platters piled high with rolls to the picnic table. Laughter, chatter and the interplay of strong personalities warmed Kay's heart. And filled her with uncertainty about how they'd react to her news.

"You would think we're feeding an army," Bobbie teased as she plopped a super-sized ketchup container on the table and then ascended the steps up to the deck.

"Our men sure can eat, and we have another mouth to feed. Did you meet Flynn yet?" Bobbie bumped her shoulder against Kay's. "I'd put *him* on my bun anytime."

Kay widened her eyes.

Bobbie laughed at Kay's expression, and then remarked, "Hell, Kay. I'm married, not dead." Instantly, tears filled Bobbie's eyes. "Oh, I'm such an ass. I'm sorry. Kay. I shouldn't have said that."

Conversations ceased as the family seemingly held their breath waiting for Kay's reaction. "Since you *are* married, I'd say you're out of the running for hot Flynn on a bun. I, on the other hand..." Kay's words lodged in her throat at the sight of Flynn, now wearing a faded CPD T-shirt, standing on the bottom step leading up to the splinter-laden deck.

"Oops, I think we forgot the mustard." Bobbie grabbed Kay's hand and giggling like a teenager, tugged her into the kitchen, Molly close behind.

"I'm so embarrassed." Kay stood at the sink and patted cold water on her flaming cheeks.

"What's to be embarrassed about?" Molly filled a glass with water and took a sip. "He's a *very* handsome man."

"Yes, he is, and I'll be working with him in two days." Kay tossed the painter's cap on the counter and ran damp hands through her spiky haircut.

"What?" Bobbie dropped the mustard bottle on the floor, luckily a plastic bottle that survived the fall. "You're going back to work? On the force?"

Bobbie scrutinized Molly's straight face. "And you knew about this, Mol, and didn't tell me."

Molly confirmed Bobbie's supposition with a nod.

"Sounds like a great idea. And what did you do to your hair? I love it." Bobbie tousled the hair on the crown of Kay's head.

"I needed a change. New hair. New job. New life. I miss Mike more than anyone can know, and I will for the rest of my life, but he would have wanted me to live and stop hiding in the house. My kids deserve better than that. I couldn't have made a change without Danny and Molly's help."

Bobbie pouted. "What help? Joe and I would have helped you if you needed us, you know."

"Danny helped me with all the paperwork, classes at the academy, and physical training. And Molly helped keep the kids fed and on schedule. I couldn't have done it without you, Molly."

"It was our pleasure to help. Danny and I agree that you're making the right career move."

"Thank you. I'm confident, too. But, not so much when it comes to the rest of my brothers' reaction to my returning to active duty."

"You'll never know until you tell them." Molly circled a bolstering arm around Kay's shoulders.

"I know. That's why I came up today. I flirted with the notion of just showing up and reporting to Pat's command on Monday. But that's too chicken." She glanced outside through the window screen, pointing her index finger. "Look at them. They act like five-year-olds sometimes."

The Sullivan brothers tossed around a bag of marshmallows, playing keep-away from Joe.

Kay's eyes shifted and she noticed Flynn, a beer in hand, standing apart from the men, abstaining from the antics. "Why is Flynn here? I thought it was just family this weekend."

"Pat called around last night to see if anyone would mind if Flynn joined us." Bobbie hefted a platter of cut fruit out from the fridge. "He lives alone, and Pat felt sorry for him. And bonus...he's great with a paintbrush."

"Odd for Pat to take in a stray. Sounds more like something Brian and Matty would do," Kay commented.

Danny entered the kitchen through the sliding glass doors. "So, Sis, are you ready to share your big news?"

Kay's heart fluttered. *New job. New life.* "Yes. I am." Taking the plunge, she marched through the door out onto the deck, her support group following behind her.

"Hey, Kay, Mom just called." Joe slipped his cell phone into his pocket.

"Mom called you, or you called her to check on our Emma?" Bobbie inquired as she brushed her hand tenderly across Joe's cheek.

Wearing his customary black eye patch, his

devilish smile reminded Kay of an unapologetic pirate. "Guilty." Joe laughed. "Anyway, Mom said everyone is just fine, and not to worry. You can stay overnight if you want, Sis."

Kay shook her head. "No, that's okay. I want to go home this evening."

"Why? Is something wrong?" Brian asked, his face concerned.

No question, her brothers truly loved her. And worried about her.

Here goes nothing. "I want to go home and organize before I start my new job on Monday."

"New job? Are you having financial problems? If you need money, we can chip in and help out," Brian asserted. Manager of the family's investments, Brian invested their money conservatively and had done well enough that they could purchase this old summer home with the profits.

"Aw, thanks for the offer, Bri," Kay said. "No, it's not money."

"Why leave the kids for a job, then?" Joe stood and walked over to Kay, touching her arm lightly. "What do you need from us?"

"I need you to please sit down and listen to me for a minute."

"Are you having some kind of breakdown?" Joe prodded. "And what did you do to your hair? You look like a punk rocker."

"I love your hair. Makes you look so young and modern," Matty declared. "Don't you think so, Charlie?"

"I agree. It looks terrific," Kay's future sister-in-law, Charlie, chimed in.

Kay smiled, grateful for her sisters' solidarity.

"Please just listen to me for a minute..." Kay paused as Flynn slipped through the sliding glass door and disappeared inside the house.

"On Monday I join the human race again." Kay

stared straight at Patrick. "I report for duty at oh-eight-hundred, sharp, Captain Sullivan."

Dead silence. Pat's mouth hung open.

Hands clenched in fists at her sides, tears brimming, Kay pleaded, "Somebody, say something."

"I am so proud of you. Congratulations." Danny practically leaped to her side.

"Absolutely. Congratulations," Charlie echoed Danny.

"Oh, from me, too," Matty proclaimed, elbowing Brian in the side.

Brian, tight-lipped, refused to comment.

"What are you, crazy?" Joe blurted out. "You think you can just wake up one morning and say, 'Gee, I want to be a police officer'?"

"You're out of line, Joe, back off," Danny cautioned, his tone brusque.

"Thanks for the vote of confidence, Joe." Kay's sarcasm deepened the scowl on Joe's face. "I have worked my ass off, figuratively and literally. I just completed the refresher course at the academy at the top of my class. So don't you dare belittle my accomplishment."

"You knew about this, Danny, and didn't think to inform *me*?" Disbelief rang in Pat's voice. "I have no paperwork, nothing. You should have warned me, Dan."

Kay's temperature, and the volume of her voice rose. "Warn you? Why should he *warn* you?"

"I'm down manpower, but I would have liked to have a say in this. Did Dad pull strings? How did you two pull this off?" Pat clearly saw this as an affront.

Infuriated, Kay declared, "You're aware of my impeccable record on the force before I had children. You all are." She glared at Pat, Joe and Brian in turn. "I was foolish enough to believe you would be happy to have me join your squad, Pat. Shame on me. Well, like it or not, Captain, I will report for duty as ordered."

Kay spun on her heel and charged into the house.

****

Flynn lit a cigarette and leaned a hip on the porch railing. He dragged hard and filled his lungs with needed nicotine. *So much for the vow to swear off smoking. Didn't even last a day.* Was Kay the reason his nervous system quaked and had him giving in to cigarette addiction? *Hot Flynn on a bun? Damn, she's hot. That spiky black hair. That toned little body.*

He took another drag and then frowned at the commotion of raised voices out back. *I must be crazy to think about Pat's sister this way. But it sounds like the little spitfire is holding her own against her brothers.*

Moments later the screen door squealed open and Kay emerged onto the porch, slamming the door with a clatter. She heaved a tray over the railing. "They think all I'm good for is baking cookies. They think *wrong.*"

Flynn watched the flat silver pan sail into Pat's front bumper with a thud. Judging from the dent in the tray, Pat would be pissed when he returned to his car.

Kay stomped over to Flynn, snatched the cigarette out of his hand and puffed deeply before she handed it back. Bent at mid-waist she hacked her brains out.

Considerately, Flynn patted her back until she caught her breath.

After her coughing fit subsided, she stood upright, sapphire eyes twinkling, and belly laughed.

"Very dramatic," she sputtered. "Obviously I'm not a smoker."

She is just adorable. Damn. Hands off, Flynn.

"You should give those up," she said, her voice less raspy.

"I'm trying to." He mouthed the cigarette and took another satisfying drag.

"Really? Doesn't look like it." Her arched eyebrows lowered. "Anyway, it's none of my business. Sorry for the fireworks display earlier."

"I couldn't help overhearing some. Everything okay now?"

"Everything is just peachy." Kay blew out a breath, grimacing. "I have thick-headed brothers who think my place is in front of the stove with a tray of cookies in each oven mitt."

"You do make great cookies." He flinched at her icy stare. Holding up both hands Flynn conceded, "Only kidding."

"Well, Captain Dowd..." Kay's lush, black eyelashes fluttered. "On Monday I'll demonstrate to you that I belong on the force as much as any of my brothers."

She stomped down the stairs and climbed into her massive SUV. The engine roared, and the gears shifted with a grind. The car screeched away. Flynn smiled and puffed on his cigarette. The light, floral scent of her perfume lingered. *Life at the stationhouse just got a whole lot more interesting.*

Chapter 2

Breathless from the tense, hour-long commute to the city and the sprint up two flights of stairs to arrive outside Pat's office at precisely eight a.m., Kay re-entered the work force, already exhausted. She hadn't slept well last night and had only managed to drift off about an hour before the buzzing alarm at five o'clock had shattered her slumber. *Why didn't I get up at four and skip sleep altogether?* The rapid-fire pace she had maintained in fixing breakfast, straightening the house, refereeing her four kids' bathroom use, packing lunches, showering and trying to look decent herself barely had allowed her to launch the SUV toward the city in time.

Tomorrow I'll develop a rhythm. At least I'm not late. Kay contemplated her new captain through the open door. Head bowed over an open file folder, he sat behind his desk, probably ignoring her. Or praying she'd go away. Kay rapped her knuckles lightly on the doorframe. "Good morning, Pat."

He raised only his blue eyes, a flinty glare. "Refer to me as Captain Sullivan, Detective Lynch," he grumbled.

Kay narrowed her eyes, but replied smoothly, "Duly noted, Captain." She lifted her right hand, holding out her paperwork toward him. "May I?"

At his nod, Kay approached her captain's desk and handed her orders to him. Without a cursory glance at their contents, Pat plopped the papers on his desk and jabbed his finger on one of the phone console's buttons. "Tom. Can you come to my office a

13

minute?"

Arms dangling, Kay requested, "May I sit?"

Mid-step she halted at Pat's retort. "No need." He stared beyond her at his office door.

A rangy man with a sandy-haired buzz cut, wearing pressed gray slacks and a starched blue pinstriped shirt, strode into the office. "Yeah, Pat?"

Apparently, formality under my brother's command only applies to me.

Pat bestowed Tom a lazy smile, and then replied, "Show the newbie to the vacant desk closest to your office." Pat pointed an index finger at Kay, wagged it back and forth between her and Tom a couple times, and said, "You two will team up for now. Start her on some of your open cases. Detective Gable, Detective Katherine Lynch."

Kay shook Gable's extended hand. "Nice to meet you, Gable."

Smiling, he responded, "It's Tom. Welcome. You're transferring in, Detective?"

Warmed by his friendly reception, Kay replied, "Please call me Kay, Tom. Actually, I'm reinstating after...my gosh, nineteen years. My son is in College of DuPage and my daughters..."

"Save the chitchat," Pat barked. "Dismissed."

"Yes, sir," Kay intoned, pleased with the lack of sarcasm in her voice. *You little shit. Lucky for you, I respect rank.*

Tom glanced at Pat and furrowed his brows. "Follow me, Kay. We'll put you to work."

Tom's rapid gait prompted Kay to scurry along abreast of her new partner. Her spirits lifted at the prospect of delving into whatever cases the man threw her way. Uneasy about how she'd strike a balance between running her household and re-establishing her career, she didn't doubt her ability to perform on the job for an instant. Pat seemed bound to make things difficult for her, but it didn't faze her. *No job is as hard as raising four kids.*

Settling in the desk chair Tom gallantly pulled out for her, Kay slipped her purse strap off her shoulder and stowed the handbag in the bottom desk drawer atop stray paperclips and a quarter inch of dust.

"I'll bring some files over. Just a sec," Tom commented, and then he strode further down the perimeter aisle, disappearing inside a gray cubicle with eight-foot-high partitions.

Her assigned desk in the humbler bullpen, facing a blank wall to boot, was an affront to her detective's rank, but that didn't bother her. *Pat can play all the games he wants. I'm here to stay.* Kay grinned. *Until I earn my own command.*

Surveying the squad room, she analyzed the population, her new co-workers and subordinates. About a quarter of the personnel were female, a bit below overall CPD averages of about thirty percent. Kay counted five women in uniform. Ten plainclothes officers wore modest makeup, minimal jewelry, slim pants, conservative blouses and blazers, similar to Kay's outfit.

Tom approached Kay's desk, a stack of file folders leaning against his chest up to his nose. Placing the two-foot-high stack on the corner of her desk, he remarked, "Tackle these 'wall' files to start. The investigations progressed over varying time periods until they hit brick walls. Fresh eyes will help."

Kay rested a hand on the top file. "Okay. No problem."

"I'll check back with you later. I have a victim's family interview on the north side."

"Want me to roll with you?"

He twisted his lips to one side. "Nah."

Kay frowned. "I'm relegated to paperwork? We're colleagues, Tom, despite this lousy work station the captain forced on me."

Tom shrugged, casual, a serene expression on his lean face. "I figured you'd appreciate easing back into the job. Plus, having a girl for a partner will take some getting used to."

Kay arched her eyebrows. "Just a minute! I'll have you know..."

Tom held up his hand, "Don't get your panties in a knot. My wife would fry my ass if I were a chauvinist. I have no problem with females on the force. Just not used to partnering, that's all. Cap hasn't assigned partners since he took over. Too many cases to cover two by two."

"Hmm. I guess he's making an exception with me."

"Yeah, well..." Tom shrugged again. "He was, uh, pretty blunt with you."

Kay sighed. "He's my brother."

Tom's lips puckered and a low whistle sounded. "You're a Sullivan?" He nodded a couple times. "Sullivan boys are good cops."

"Thanks." Kay beamed. "I was the first Sullivan *boy* on the force. It's the only job, outside of motherhood, I've ever held."

Tom tapped a finger on his forehead, a buzz-cut salute. "Well, Katie Sullivan. I guess we have officially joined forces. Check back with you later."

"Sounds good." Kay tapped the stack of case files. "Plenty to keep me occupied."

Discovering a dog-eared yellow legal pad and a ballpoint pen in the center drawer, she tackled Gable's "brick wall." Bent over her work, Kay immersed herself in case details: interview transcripts, victims' photos, coroners' reports, investigative detours, and dead ends. Ambient conversations hummed dimly in her subconscious like a hive's drone of incoherent syllables. Phones bleated. Faint whiffs of aftershaves, perfumes, and the tang of body odor drifted on the air. She hardly raised her head as she consecutively transferred files from the left side of the desk, spread them open in the center for review, and then stacked them to her right after finishing. Piles shifted dimensions from left to right like an hourglass marking time.

Barring a meandering trip in search of a restroom and a quickly gobbled granola bar at her desk, Kay plodded through files. Pages of notes multiplied with little import other than to document Kay's understanding of each case's status. Her fresh eyes hadn't detected fresh avenues of pursuit until one case snagged her attention, maybe because her thoughts occasionally strayed to her kids.

The victim was a toddler: Darla Irving. COD, a crushed windpipe from blunt trauma. Beaten to death. The victim's photo depicted a rosy-cheeked face, bloodied and misshapen; the tiny body slumped in a high chair, cheery gingham kitchen curtains in the background. Kay's heart twisted.

She rifled through the pages in the thick folder, counting ten 911 dispatches of cruisers in the past year to the victim's home on domestic abuse complaints by Connie Irving, the toddler's mother, against her husband, Dennis Irving. Photos of Connie sporting black eyes and busted lips abounded, but she had refused to lodge formal complaints in all instances, and the wife beater had remained at liberty to bust lips at will.

Her attention riveted, Kay concentrated on the incident report from the day of the toddler's murder three months ago. 911 transcripts of Connie Irving's hysteria resulted in documentation of disjointed one-word screams: Fists. Kill. Her. Help. At the scene, paramedics were dispatched to intake the battered Connie Irving. Another van was dispatched to transport Darla Irving's lifeless body. Dennis Irving had rabbited, and an APB remained outstanding for his arrest.

After Connie Irving had been discharged from the hospital the next morning, her fractured hand in a cast, her face crisscrossed with stitches on multiple lacerations, an investigative team, led by Gable, disposed of a search warrant for the Irving home and interviewed Mrs. Irving. Distraught, nearly catatonic, the mother described her husband's fury, and her inability to protect her child from his swinging fists—again, documented as one-word bursts. She had shadowed the search team's progress from room to room, had sat in a kitchen chair across from the high chair in the victim's photo for an hour while the team had worked, but had refused to enter her daughter's room during the search.

Bundling the contents of the file with two hands, Kay squared off the papers with a couple taps on the desktop and then leafed through each page again, concentrating on the record of subsequent phone conversations with Connie Irving since the death of her daughter.

Kay glanced up as Tom Gable breezed behind her. "How's it goin', Katie boy?" he teased.

Grinning, Kay rubbed her stiff neck. "Do you have a minute to discuss the Darla Irving homicide?"

"Yeah, sure." Tom dragged a chair over and straddled it, facing Kay.

"Is your filing on this case up to date?" Kay inquired, folder in hand.

"Yep. You think something's missing?"

"Maybe. I'd like to bring Connie Irving in for further questioning. Do you have any objection?"

"No. But I think we already have our perp. The APB just has to yield the husband," Tom opined.

"Do you remember the day of the search? Anything Connie Irving said that isn't documented?"

"Are you kidding? Her mouth was swollen to the

size of a catcher's mitt and she couldn't say much. The woman was broken all over."

"I'd like to talk to her. Do you want to be present?"

Chair legs scraped linoleum. Gable stood upright. "You can handle it. One case I don't have to think about. Knock yourself out. Plenty more where that came from." Gable winked and walked away from her.

"Line four for Katherine Lynch!" a deep voice hollered. "Who the hell is Katherine Lynch?"

"That's me." Kay raised her left arm, and punched the line button on her phone with her right hand, picked up the handset. "Kay Lynch," she said.

"Mrs. Lynch, this is the school nurse at Arbor Elementary. Peggy is with me, complaining of an upset stomach. She wants to go home."

Kay's stomach clenched. *Give me a break, baby. It's my first day.* "Uh..." Kay glanced at her watch. "It's already past one. Can't she manage until dismissal?"

"I'm afraid not," the woman asserted. "She insists."

Kay huffed a breath. "Can you please put her on the phone?"

Shuffling, a muffled voice, as the phone changed hands. "Momma," Peggy whined. "My tummy hurts."

"I'm so sorry, baby," Kay soothed. "But Mommy's working. Mary will be there as soon as the dismissal bell rings. She can give you some Coke when you get home."

"I want to go home *now*," her daughter wailed.

"Okay, okay..." Kay's mind reeled. *Where is Mary with her day? What did she tell me this morning?*

"Momma, are you *coming*?" Peggy insisted.

I think Mary has an exam. Shit. "Of course, sweetheart. Tell the nurse I'm on my way. And you rest until I get there."

Dumping the handset back in the console, Kay shoved her chair back and stalked to Patrick's office. Empty. Her back to his office door, Kay scanned the squad room searching for her commanding officer. She didn't see him, so she ducked into his office and scribbled a note:

Be back in about an hour. Kay

Folding the slip of paper in half, she tossed the note on his chair seat, and fled the squad room.

Tempting the fates that she'd receive a speeding ticket on her first day as a duly sworn police officer, Kay rocketed down the Eisenhower Expressway bound for the Arbor Village exit.

Depressing the call icon on the steering wheel, Kay commanded, "Dial Mary."

A string of bleeps sounded as the system dialed the number, three rings and Mary's voicemail greeting played, followed by a beep.

"Hey, sweetie, it's Mom. I'm on my way to school to pick up Peggy. She has a stomachache. I'll take her back to work with me. Can you please come pick her up at the station when you're done with school? It's Uncle Pat's office on State. *My office.* Thanks."

****

Towing Peggy by the hand, Kay entered the squad room. Nobody seemed to notice, or presumably care, that the newbie strolled the aisle with an eight-year-old. A gleeful, completely healthy eight-year-old, Kay estimated.

Accelerating the pace to speed past Pat's open office door, Kay thought she was home free until she heard, "Detective!" boom from the captain's lair.

Reversing, Kay stepped in front of his doorway, Peggy's hand warm in hers.

"Hi ya, Uncle Pat," Peggy sang. "Mommy brought me to her work."

"Hey there, pumpkin," Pat responded, a broad

smile on his handsome face. "Come give Uncle Pat a hug."

Pat enveloped his niece in a brawny embrace, his eyes shooting daggers at Kay over Peggy's glossy blonde crown.

Chapter 3

"What do you think, Momma? Does this look like Uncle Pat?" Kay blinked at the stick figure masterpiece Peggy slid across the desktop.

"It looks just like him. I think Uncle Pat will love it, honey."

"It's not finished yet." Peggy reclaimed the paper, skimming it over the desk sideways, and bent her towhead over it as she colored the oversized shield on the stick figure's chest. Her pink tongue protruding at the corner of her mouth, she carefully printed "Peggy Lynch" on the bottom corner of the page, the finishing touch.

"All done." Her innocent smile tugged at Kay's heart. "I signed it like a real artist. That's what I am going to be when I grow up. Is it okay for me to show it to Uncle Pat, Momma?"

Kay eyed Pat's office door, hanging ajar. "Uncle Pat is very busy today. Let me take it to him. While I'm gone, why don't you start a new picture?" She placed a fresh piece of paper in front of Peggy and headed to her brother's office.

Pat did not react to her light tap on the door, seemingly transfixed on the paperwork spread on his desk.

"Captain Sullivan, may I come in?"

He nodded, but didn't look up.

"I'm sorry I had to run to the school to pick up Peggy. I rushed back. Didn't take a lunch break today..."

"Unacceptable, Detective Lynch."

"Excuse me?" Hands on her hips, she moved

22

through the doorway and planted her feet in front of his desk.

"I said your behavior today is unacceptable. If you go off duty again without permission, I will be forced to write you up."

Tamping down the urge to slam the door with a full arm swing, Kay closed it quietly instead. No need to broadcast her dressing down to the squad room at large.

"Pat, I had no choice. I called Mary, but she didn't answer. She had an exam today. What was I supposed to do?" She hated her plaintive tone, the way her voice trembled.

"Your personal life has no place in my department."

"Come on, Pat. I had to leave *temporarily*. Peggy needed me."

"I will not remind you again to address me as *Captain* in this office." He picked a file off his desk, clutched it in his big mitt, and swiveled toward his credenza, leaving her to stare at the back of his head. *Dismissed.*

"Captain," she barked, venom dripping, "I apologize, sir. What exactly is the proper procedure to avoid infraction when called away from the building on an emergency?"

Captain *asshole* Patrick faced her now, his lips a grim line, his blue eyes dispassionate. "It was hardly an emergency." He snorted, then leaned to the right, glancing past Kay. A smile lit his face as he waved his hand.

Confused, Kay twisted her neck to follow his line of sight. The glass in the office door framed Peggy's adorable face, all cheer and pink cheeks, beaming at her uncle with characteristic hero worship.

Kay's soft smile bloomed while regarding her daughter, but her brother's cold demeanor effectively banished the smile when she turned face front and regarded her captain instead.

"Peggy looks perfectly fine to me," Pat declared, his speech clipped.

Kay wanted to wipe that smug look off his face. *Didn't he appreciate what that little girl had gone through? How she might perceive Kay's decision to return to work, having experienced her father's abandonment in death?* She would not give Pat the satisfaction of undermining her or questioning her professional ability because of any personal considerations. Tears threatened, but Kay would be damned if she'd let her snot-nosed baby brother see her break down, her first day back on the job. *Screw you, Patrick.*

"My private life will not interfere in your department again, sir. Please note that I spent forty-five minutes of my lunch hour handling a personal problem, and according to union law I have fifteen minutes due me, which I will take when my other daughter arrives to escort this one home. In the future, I will not report on my activities during said lunch hour, personal or otherwise."

"Well, Detective Lynch. Nice bluff, spouting union rules to me." Pat crossed one leg, his kneecap jutting above the edge of his desk. He tented his hands over his knee. "The union provides for thirty-minute lunch breaks. Although you're not required to report on your activities during said break, you *are* required to report when you leave service and when you are available for service again."

Kay's eyes involuntarily closed, cheeks flaming. She breathed deeply, and then looked at his face, her eyes narrowed to slits. "Understood. Thank you for your time, Captain."

She backed up a few steps, prepared to about-face in military style and get the hell out of there.

Pat thrust out a hand, palm up. "Is that for me?"

Kay lowered her eyes, surveying Peggy's

drawing. Slowly folding the paper in quarters, she locked her eyes on his as she slid the paper into her slacks pocket. "No, sir. You don't deserve it."

Executing that about-face now, Kay opened the door and stomped out, straight into Flynn Dowd's chest.

Strong hands on her shoulders steadied Kay's stance. "Hey, lady." Flynn grinned, green eyes twinkling. "How's your first day going?"

"Just peachy." Kay scooted around him and marched to her desk, a smile plastered on her face for her daughter's benefit.

"Did Uncle Pat like his picture?" Her little girl bit her nail and searched Kay's face, her expression expectant, heartbreaking.

"You bet he did, honey. He loved it." Kay plopped into her chair and fumed, staring at Flynn's back, his long muscular body leaning against the doorframe of Pat's office. Hearty male laughter and bass voices boomed. Her mind raced as Flynn and her brother joked and had a swell time.

Why is Pat doing this to me? Doesn't he have any idea how hard today is for my children and me? Is it wrong to expect a little understanding from my own brother?

Emerald green eyes met hers when Flynn left Pat's office. He shrugged his shoulders and smiled. *What the hell did Pat say to him?*

Kay dipped her eyes toward her computer screen, pointedly ignoring Flynn. When she gauged it safe, she hazarded a glance upward and watched him leave the squad room. *That man has me all...twitchy.*

Relief flooded through Kay's over-stressed system as her daughter Mary entered the squad room.

"Mom!" Mary called.

"Sweetie, thank you so much for coming so

quickly." Kay jumped up and hugged Mary tight, comfort flooding her.

"No prob, Mom. What's the matter, Pegster, your tummy hurts?"

"Yes, my tummy hurts real bad. Nurse Zeitler called Momma, and she came and got me."

"That's too bad. I was going to make popcorn at home later, but I guess I better not. I don't want your tummy ache to get worse," Mary said.

"It's feeling much better now." Peggy stuffed the half-colored drawing into her backpack and tossed in a fistful of crayons. "Can we watch a movie, too?"

Stomach ache miraculously cured, Peggy popped up from her chair and grasped Mary's hand.

"Sure we can, Pegster. I'll even let you pick the movie." Mary squeezed Peggy's shoulder affectionately.

"Seriously, I can't thank you enough, Mary," Kay professed.

"Really, Mom. It's nothing. I'm so proud of you. Look at all you have accomplished." Mary swept her left arm back and forth in front of her, pointing out the world of the bustling squad room that Kay now inhabited. "Back on the job. I bet Uncle Pat is happy to have you here. Where is he? Can I say hello?"

"I think Uncle Pat is in a meeting. Let's not bother him. I'll tell him you said hello." Kay saw no reason to permit her difficulties with her captain to damage the close relationship her children had with her brother. After Mike died, *all* her brothers had encircled her children with their love, Pat included. She would never forget how they had helped her kids heal from the horror of losing their daddy. *I just wish Pat would support me now.*

"I'll walk you girls to the car," Kay volunteered as she hoisted Peggy's backpack over her shoulder and ushered her girls to the elevator.

Creaky hisses as the scuffed, dirt-smudged

elevator doors slid closed. Kay kissed Mary's soft cheek and then inquired, "How was school today?"

"Same as any other day." Mary's smile brightened her face. Pale freckles dotted her nose and fair cheeks. Golden tendrils of hair escaped the ponytail and curled around her heart-shaped face. Mike's crystal blue eyes stared back at her. Mary, of her four children, resembled the Lynch side of the family. The twins and Mike Jr. were Sullivan through and through.

"Mikey said he would pick up Malnati's pizzas and salad on his way home tonight, so I don't have to cook for the troops yet," Mary informed Kay as they exited the elevator bound for the parking lot.

"You know he doesn't like to be called Mikey anymore. Try to call him Mike," Kay requested, opening the rear door of Mary's car, a powder blue compact amid a sea of black cruisers and hulking, police-issue SUVs.

Peggy tromped in front of Kay and settled on the car seat.

"I remember to call him Mike most of the time. Don't worry." Mary reached into the backseat, snapped Peggy's seatbelt in place, and closed the door.

Tears brimmed in Kay's eyes. *What would I do without my kids?* She swiped the tears off her cheeks, a dull ache lingering in her chest. The sun dipped low in the clear blue sky, a couple hours away from dusk. Kay yearned for the old rhythms, the comfortable routine that had marked her life as a stay-at-home mom.

The T-shirt tucked into Mary's slim jeans refocused Kay's attention, and she laughed.

"Have you and Amy stopped fighting yet?" Kay pointed to Mary's shirt bearing the TEAM EDWARD imprint. Inseparable friends since grade school, Mary and Amy had become family when Kay's brother Danny had married Amy's mother, Molly. Lately they warred incessantly, each entrenched in the "Edward" or "Jacob" camp.

"Let's just say we have agreed to disagree," Mary replied. "I mean, come on, Mom. You watched *Twilight* with me."

"Yes, at least three times." Kay chuckled.

"Well, duh, Mom. Team Jacob? I don't think so. What does Amy see in Jacob? Edward is…well, he is Edward."

Lord, yes. Edward is definitely Edward.

"As long as you girls stop fighting. That's all I care about."

Mary kissed her mother's cheek. "We've ceased fire, Detective Mom." Flashing a perfect smile, Mary rounded the car bumper. "See you at home."

"Be careful driving."

"Always am." Mary opened the driver's door and grinned.

"And make sure you give the twins something nutritious for an after-school snack," Kay added.

"I've got your back, Mom. Go get the bad guys."

Mary's sunny blonde head dipped below the roofline of the car. The car door clunked and the engine fired.

Mary drove at a snail's pace toward the lot exit, Kay strolling behind the car. When there was a break in the steady traffic, Mary accelerated and steered onto the street. Filled with doubts, Kay trained her eyes on the receding taillights until the car turned the corner and disappeared from view. *Why isn't my family enough? Why can't I be happy staying home, taking care of them? Am I wrong to want something for myself?* She pulled a crumpled tissue out of her pocket and blew her nose.

The smell of cigarette smoke permeated the air. Flynn leaned against the building, his eyes locked on her. Embarrassed, she dug her hands deep in her pants pockets and approached him.

"Thought you were giving those up," Kay remarked as she neared him.

"Want a drag?" His eyes crinkled with his sly grin.

"No, thanks." She laughed remembering her coughing fit.

"Having a tough first day?" He tossed the half-smoked cigarette to the sidewalk and ground it under his boot.

"Yes. My daughter had an apparent phantom stomach ache. It magically disappeared the minute I picked her up from school."

"I remember when we first moved to our new house, Flynnie had my wife or me at school at least once a week for a month. Change scares the daylights out of kids." His eyes clouded.

"You're married?" *Damn, all that wasted daydreaming.*

"I was. I'm a widower."

Empathy swelled inside Kay. "I'm so sorry. How is your son dealing with it?"

Flynn didn't respond and lowered his eyes. Kay's conscience pricked at her apparent social gaffe. *I should know better than to blurt out personal questions about grief.*

"I lost them both the same day. A stolen car, police chase," Flynn divulged, fixing a steady gaze on Kay, a well of sadness in his eyes.

Kay's stomach dove in sympathy, and she expelled a long breath on a sigh.

"Ironic, isn't it? I was supposed to pick Flynnie up from baseball practice, but I manned the roadblock we had set up to capture the punk who stole the car that killed my wife and son. I wish I had picked up my son. I would give anything to be the one who died in that car with him."

The familiar stab of pain assaulted Kay. "I

know. I lie in bed at night and rewind it all in my mind so that the drunk driver slams into *my* car and kills me instead of my husband. Not that I want to die. It's just so damn hard without him." She shook her head, extracted her hands from her pockets and dragged her fingers through her hair.

Flynn reached out and clasped her hand. "You are the first person who didn't try to placate me. If I hear, 'Flynn, don't say that. Be happy you are alive,' one more time..." His penetrating eyes locked on hers. "You understand, don't you?"

"I do. When did this happen?" Kay squeezed his hand thinking to encourage him, deriving tremendous comfort herself from the warmth of his hand around hers.

"Four years ago."

"I never heard about it."

"No reason you would. It happened back home in New Jersey. I stuck it out at my precinct for a couple of years, but each day got harder. Too many reminders. I made a clean break over a year ago."

"Are you happy in Chicago?" *For the first time in a long time, I'm happy holding a man's hand.*

"I'm getting there." A melancholy smile dimpled his cheeks. His eyes bored into hers, unreadable. Tantalizing.

A rush of pure chemical attraction streamed through Kay. "I'm glad," she whispered.

"A guy could fall for a girl like you." His thumb pressed gently under each of her eyes, brushing away tears Kay hadn't realized she'd shed until now.

Her peripheral vision blurred, a lovely haze where only his sparkling emerald eyes held her focus. Kay clasped his wrist in her trembling hand. "A girl could fall for a guy like you."

The hands on his silver, chunky wristwatch diverted Kay. "*Holy shit.* Is that the time?"

Flynn flinched and furrowed his brow. "Have an

appointment?"

"I'm dead if Pat notices I've been away from the desk this long," Kay explained as she dropped his arm and headed to the door.

"Don't worry about your captain." Flynn held the door open and Kay pounded up the stairs, leaving Flynn behind.

"Easy for you to say," she tossed out. "You don't have to report to the man."

At the landing, Kay stopped a second to catch her breath, and then yanked the door to squad room open. Pat stood, scanning the vicinity just outside his office door.

"Detective Lynch," Flynn pronounced behind her, his deep voice projecting like a stage actor's. "When you have a minute, stop by my office so we can review the file I was discussing with you."

Grateful...*Eternally grateful...* Kay turned as Flynn continued down the hall.

"I will, Captain, thank you," she replied in a loud voice.

Disregarding Pat's presence, Kay prayed he wouldn't ask what case Flynn referred to while she traversed the squad room, sat at her desk, and opened a file. Her hands shook. When she dared a glance at her brother's office, relief flooded at the sight of him behind his desk. She owed Captain Flynn Dowd, and relished the prospect of repaying him somehow.

I could fall for a guy like him.
****

Man, this place stinks. Don't these old bastards take a bath before they put on their Santa suits? The open locker releases an even worse odor. Eyes watering, I wave my glove in front of my face, but it's too late. The camphor-laden stench of mothballs gags me, reminds me of him. Looming over me, his clothes always reeked of that nauseating stuff. Nightmare memories invade again.

His belt lashed through the air and the smell of mothballs filled my nose. "Don't, Father! I'll be good. I promise I won't do it again..."

"You're doing nothing, as usual. Sitting on the porch in the middle of the day? Idle hands are the devil's playthings!" he roared as the snake of leather slashed my back. Pain shot down my legs.

Father worked around the clock. Creepy bastard never slept. No sneakin' out to parties for me.

"You'll go help your mother this instant! And you'll remember to do as I tell you, or there'll be more of this!" That time the belt broke the skin on my forearm. Still have the scar.

I did what I was told. I learned to be good. God, I was good.

I blink and my mind clears. They're no different than Father.

Get to work.

Easing the locker door shut without a sound, I'm satisfied. Drink up that whole thermos, Santa Claus. Do as you're told. Now I give the orders.

Dashing through the snow
In a one-horse, open sleigh,
Little do they know,
Death is on its way...

Chapter 4

Kay delayed knocking on Flynn's office door, preferring to watch him at work behind his desk while unaware. Longish black hair, streaked with a few white strands, framed a face boyish but for the smattering of laugh lines around his eyes. The musky scent of leather radiated into the hallway.

He raised his long-lashed emerald eyes and bestowed Kay with a welcoming smile that creased those merry lines around his eyes and dimpled his cheeks. "Here to go over that file I conjured out of thin air last week to save you from a reprimand?"

Grinning, Kay took a seat in front of his desk. "I'm very thankful you mentioned that file to cover for me, Flynn. Pat was crouched in the bushes, ready to pounce on any so-called infraction." Cramped in the small space on the only chair except for his, she basked in the smell of his lust-provoking aftershave.

"Actually, I have a real case here." She brushed her hand over the file folder nestled in her lap. "Battered wife, child beaten to death. The husband and father is the prime suspect. Still at large. Something's not fitting with me. I'd like to run it by you, if you're interested in consulting on the case?"

"Sure. What's your slant?" He leaned forward at the waist, elbows on his desk, his eyes narrowed.

Flynn's intent concentration on her spurred heart-racing distraction. Her temperature spiked with her pulse and her cheeks flamed. But Kay had sought out Flynn today solely for his professional opinion about her case. The primal reactions unleashed by the mere thought of him lately had her examining her possible personal agenda with the district's profiler.

Business first.

"The case involves a history of multiple incidents of domestic abuse. Dennis Irving beat Connie Irving repeatedly. Three months ago, he apparently beat her again and then turned his fists on their fourteen-month-old daughter, Darla, resulting in her death," Kay summarized. "Investigators at the scene reported that Connie was unwilling to enter her daughter's room, yet she sat in the kitchen, the scene of her daughter's murder, without complaint. Follow up calls from Connie since then concerned obtaining permission from investigators to clean out her daughter's room and 'get rid of her things.' That behavior puzzles me. Isn't it more common for a parent, especially a mother, to wish to preserve a lost child's room exactly?"

****

A lost child. A dead child. My Flynnie.

Flynn had cultivated the discipline long ago to separate casework, so often associated with death, and his personal experience...outwardly.

"Yes," Flynn replied, his tone even, neutral. "In the overwhelming majority of cases, parents tend to enshrine a dead child's things, his..." Flynn cleared his throat. "Or her room, as a way of holding on. Parting with a child's belongings and clearing out the room the child occupied are usually preceded by years of grief resolution."

Kay nodded her head, her eyes downcast, apparently pondering his behavioral evaluation.

Picking up a pencil and tapping its eraser against the desk blotter rhythmically, Flynn studied her.

"I thought so," she concluded.

He respected the blazing intelligence in her sky-blue eyes, appreciated her spirit and determination. During their limited interactions, he'd found her laughter contagious, her frequent lightheartedness addictive. Her simple touch reawakened his numbed senses, loosened ironclad restraint and enlivened his spirit. *Hell, I even like her hair, despite her brothers' horror that she ditched natural blonde for black.*

"Also, she never inquired if we'd caught her husband yet, when she phoned," Kay added. "That doesn't necessarily mean anything, since we'd call her if he were apprehended. Still. Doesn't jibe."

Flynn nodded. "I agree."

Kay had assumed a fantasy role in his mind recently. *That sexy, toned body. Her willingness to stand up to the men in her family with courage and conviction. She could probably deck one or the other of them with one punch.*

Patrick remained determined to stall her career. *Good luck with that, Pat.*

Her compassion and understanding of Flynn's unbearable loss had established their common ground, fresh ground...had him contemplating candlelit dinners, silky skin beneath his skimming fingers, mind-blanking flights of lovemaking...

"Care to take a ride with me?" Wide-eyed, Kay poised at the edge of her chair.

"Huh?"

"To interview Connie Irving?" She stared at him. "Haven't you been listening?"

"Sorry." He glanced at his calendar. "Now?"

Kay stood, smiling. "If you're free."

"Sure." Flynn rose, slipping his blazer off the back of his chair. He shrugged it on and circled his desk.

Kay opted to drive, so Flynn opened the driver door before he rounded the car and took the passenger seat. Switching the ignition on, Kay commented, "No smoking in the cruiser. The kids like to sit in it—don't tell Pat—and if it reeks of smoke they'll think the *new me* has gone straight to hell." She chuckled.

"I really am quitting. This will make it mandatory for the time being." Flynn wedged his hand between the side of his seat and the door to change his seat's position, gaining a few more inches of legroom. "How are they adjusting to your work schedule?"

Kay smiled as she maneuvered the car out of the lot. "They're amazing, thanks for asking. And Mom and my sisters-in-law help out, too. I'm very blessed."

Flynn relaxed, content to let her wrestle with city traffic. "Where are we going?"

"Wrigleyville. Shouldn't take long," Kay said.

"Things better with Pat now?"

"Ha!" Kay merged onto Lake Shore Drive. "I keep my distance, nose to the grindstone. This case was originally Tom Gable's. Tom gave me carte blanche to work it, so I'm working it. Thanks for your help."

"Glad to oblige." To Flynn's right, Lake Michigan met the shore. As the car sped, a blur of intense blue color streamed by the car window like an unfurling, shimmering ribbon. "Do you need me to contribute anything specific to this interview?"

Eyes focused on the road, Kay steered down the exit ramp. "Feel free to jump in. I think I know where I'm going with this, though."

****

Seated at Connie Irving's kitchen table, the introductions behind them, Flynn remained highly interested in observing Kay's interrogation style and witnessing how she applied her investigative instincts.

The small room was clean and obviously well maintained. Formica countertops and older, mustard yellow appliances gleamed. Connie Irving, thin, almost skeletal, deep circles under her eyes, had an air of overwork to exhaustion about her.

"Mrs. Irving, my condolences on your loss," Kay remarked. "Reliving the circumstances of your daughter's death must be extremely painful. I apologize for the need to bring up these excruciating matters again, but as I mentioned on the phone, I have a few questions."

"All right." Connie Irving's eyes seemed sunken, ringed with dark shadows. "What do you want to know?"

"How is your hand mending?" Kay pointed to the ACE bandage wrapped around Connie's hand and forearm.

"It still swells up." Dull-eyed, Connie stared at her hand. "Hurts like hell when it does."

"On the night your hand was injured," Kay continued, "why did you refuse to enter your daughter's bedroom?"

"Did I? I don't remember that," Connie responded, her voice a monotone.

Kay glanced toward the kitchen window. "I notice you removed the highchair from this room. Have you cleaned out Darla's bedroom since then? Uh, gotten rid of your daughter's things?" Kay thumbed through papers in a manila file. "You requested permission to do that several times."

"Yes." Connie nodded her head, her face expressionless.

"Is the room empty? May I see it?" Kay shifted to the edge of her chair as if to stand.

"I guess." Connie shrugged her shoulders. "I turned the room back into a study. Like before she was born. My Denny always loved that study."

"I see." Kay closed the file and placed it on the kitchen table with exaggerated care. "Mrs. Irving, how did you injure your hand?"

"What?" Alarm flickered in her brown eyes before she lowered them, seemingly staring at the table's edge. "Don't you have all that in the file? My husband beat me. I called 911. There must be records."

Kay folded her hands and leaned them on the table. "Aren't you curious if we've found your husband? You've never asked."

"Did you?" Her eyes widened and then narrowed, tracking rapidly back and forth.

Flynn worked to interpret her body language. *No desire for vengeance. Hopeful?*

"What if we have? Will you be glad to testify against him?" Flynn inquired, intuiting Kay's direction with this, his inflections casual, conversational.

"What? No. He didn't mean it. He never means it, you know." Connie wrung her hands and then tugged a strand of stringy brown hair.

Kay tensed next to him. "He didn't break your hand, did he?"

"No...I mean, yes." Connie wagged her head. "He kept punching, punching. Darla wailed. I was crying, screaming. Trying to make him stop."

"He did stop, didn't he?" Kay leaned forward, her torso angled over the tabletop. "He stopped hitting you, and he left. He left you alone with a screaming baby. And you shut her up. Just like he wanted you to do since the day she was born. But she never would shut up. So he hit you, punished you. You wanted things to go back to the way they were before she was born. And that night, you shut her up for good. Didn't you, Connie?"

"Stop it, stop it!" Connie covered her ears, eyes pinched closed. "You're confusing me. He wouldn't stop! You stop. You stop now!" she screamed.

Kay shoved her chair back and stood. Her palms on the table, she leaned forward, straight-armed, in

Connie's face. "What if we have your husband in custody right now?"

"The burly guy Gable brought in yesterday?" Flynn tossed out. "I didn't make the connection until now."

"Exactly." Kay straightened, paced a few steps. "We'll charge him with murder in the first degree whether you testify or not." Kay approached the table and tapped the file with her hand. "We have it all in here. Photos. A long string of beating incidents *you* reported."

Kay rounded the table and dragged her chair directly in front of Connie's. She sat and leaned forward within inches from Connie's face. "He'll go to prison. Look at me, Connie," Kay demanded. "Do you know what inmates do to baby killers?"

A roar sounded, more animal than human. A man charged into the room, barreling into Kay's chair from behind. The momentum crashed Kay's body into Connie's, hurling both women onto the floor and jutting the table edge into Flynn's midriff.

Flynn shoved the table away from him. His chair flew into the cabinets behind him with the backward flex of his thigh muscles.

The man swept Kay off the floor with one arm, carrying her forward in a football tuck. He shifted her in midair as if she were weightless, so that she hung over his thickly muscled arm at the waist, her body dangling like a shield in front of him. In seconds, he barreled to a dead end at the kitchen counter, clasped the hilt of a butcher knife, and yanked it free from the wood block.

Kay's legs bicycled in air, kicking the man's knees and shins. He jerked his forearm against her waist and swung her forward, a pendulum's arc. Her feet slapped the floor on the downswing and the man tightened his hold on her, pinioning her against his chest, the knife at her throat.

Instinctively Flynn crossed his right hand over his chest to draw from his shoulder holster. The split-second awareness that his gun was in his desk drawer had him holding his hands lax at his sides, facing the intruder. "I'm not armed, Denny. You don't want to hurt her. You *are* Denny Irving, correct?"

"Get up off the floor," he bellowed, malice gleaming in the hazel eyes he cast at Connie Irving. She quivered in a fetal position on the floor, both hands clasping the nape of her neck.

Kay's eyes met Flynn's. Relief coursed through him at her calm expression, despite the rapid expansion and contraction of her chest beneath the man's muscled arm. "Connie, he'll kill you just like he killed your baby," Kay pronounced, her breath labored.

"*What?*" Denny bellowed. "*Killed?* You didn't give her over to welfare people like you told me? Get up, you useless piece of shit. I said *get up!*" He jostled Kay herky-jerky during his outraged rant.

Kay's chin dipped deeply toward her chest, perilously over the knife's blade, and then she whipped her head backward butting Denny's nose with a sharp crack. His eyes rolled back, his irises disappearing. Seizing his wrist with both hands, Kay twisted with opposing motion, as if she were opening a double-lidded jar, and the knife clattered to the floor. Clasping both her hands in front of her chest, she speared the point of her elbow into Denny's windpipe like a battering ram.

The man toppled, a resounding thud on the linoleum. If the windpipe blow hadn't knocked the breath out of him, the flat-backed landing did the trick. Kay drew her gun from the shoulder holster, tossed it to Flynn, and lunged toward Denny's prone body. She grabbed his shoulders and heaved him into a roll onto his stomach. Fishing one-handed in her jacket, Kay extracted a pair of cuffs and in two quick moves secured the man's hands behind his back. She stood and beamed at Flynn. A hairline cut on the side of her neck trickled blood. Already an angry welt on her forehead discolored her fair skin bluish.

Flynn smiled. Shaking his head, he handed Kay her gun. "I was completely useless."

"Not if you have a set of cuffs on you," Kay replied, holstering her weapon and motioning toward Connie, still cowering on the floor.

"Yes, ma'am." Flynn tossed her the cuffs, impressed with her nonchalant, one-handed catch.

Flynn's heart somersaulted in his chest. *Pat Sullivan, your sister is here to stay.*

Kay tapped Connie's shoulder. "Connie, you have to come with me now."

The woman lifted her head in response, twisting her neck to look up at Kay.

"Keep your hands behind you, please," Kay commanded as she fastened the cuffs. "Connie Irving, you have the right to remain silent…"

****

"Cap, you have a minute?" Tom Gable asked, halting outside Pat's office, Kay at his side.

"Sure." Pat's eyes turned suspicious when Kay followed Gable into his office. "Hello, Lynch."

Kay acknowledged Pat with a nod. "Captain."

Gable grasped the back of a chair and inched it back a few inches. "Have a seat, Katie."

Pat regarded him quizzically. "Katie?"

Gable grinned. "I call her 'Katie boy.' Because Sullivan boys are great cops."

Pat raised one eyebrow in unspoken opinion, a trick Kay could never master. *Little snot.*

Gable sat on the other chair in front of Pat's desk. "And she earned it. Cap, I'm officially requesting a commendation for Katie here. She collared Dennis and Connie Irving. Figured out motive and extracted a confession of murder from Connie Irving with Captain Flynn Dowd as witness. Neat as a pin. Couldn't have done better myself."

Kay's heart leaped. *Gable, I think I love you.*

Pat had stared at Kay steadily while Gable spoke, his flashing blue eyes at odds with the neutral expression on his face. "And the paperwork is where?"

Kay handed over the file. "It's complete, Captain."

Pat accepted the file, opened it, and scanned the first page quickly.

"Captain Dowd also submitted a report of his opinion after our initial consultation on the case, a transcript of the interviews before and after Connie Irving's arrest, and a situation report of Dennis Irving's assault and subsequent arrest," Kay recited, her head high, her lips twitching to restrain a full-blown grin.

Pat raised his head and pushed back from his desk. Still straight-faced, he extended his right hand.

Kay rose and clasped it, beaming.

"Good work, Detective," Pat said delivering a bruising handshake. "Tom, write the commendation request up for my review."

Chapter 5

Coffee sloshed over the rim of Kay's mug as she rushed to her desk, splattering her hand and the crisp, white blouse she wore. *Damn it. Monday mornings suck.* Plopping down on her desk chair, she used a tissue to blot out the offending brown stain. She smeared it instead, enlarging the mud-colored blemish more. *Shit.* Kay pitched the soggy tissue in the wastebasket.

The weekend had flown. *Wasn't it* just *Friday?* By the time Kay had cleaned the house, shopped for groceries, prepared dinners for the week, disposed of mounds of wash and ironing, and cheered on the Bears it was, somehow, Sunday night. *Another week. Another drama.* This morning Amanda had complained of a stomach ache.

Thank God, Mom and Dad are back from Florida until after Thanksgiving. The senior Sullivans would stay with Kay through the holidays. Amanda could spend the day cocooned in her grandparents' love, and Kay could focus on her job.

Kay removed several files from her briefcase and placed them in a tidy pile on her desk. Filled with good intentions Friday evening, she had carried them home to review over the weekend, but her briefcase had remained unopened until now. The top folder caught her attention. She rose and ducked into Tom Gable's cubicle, hoping to discuss her theory about the case with him before the scheduled squad meeting. But he wasn't at his desk.

Toting her third cup of coffee, this time a partially filled mug, Kay trailed several colleagues into the meeting room. Chairs scraped on the linoleum and casual chatter filled the room. Kay loved the camaraderie of the group. With four cold cases closed due to her diligence, Kay slowly had earned their respect.

Selecting a second row aisle seat in the front third of the room, she waited for the meeting to commence, her mind pleasantly blank. Ten minutes beyond the appointed time, Pat, his muscular six-foot-six stature imposing, marched to the front of the room. Conversations cut off like a flipped switch. He placed his notes on the lectern, eyes downcast, auburn hair gleaming under the fluorescent lights. Raising his eyes, he smiled at the group at large.

"Good morning. Sorry for the delay. I was on the phone with the mayor. Let's get started." Patrick referred occasionally to a list as he spoke, methodically checking off items with a ballpoint pen.

After handing out several assignments, Pat glanced at Kay's partner and asked, "Detective Gable, anything on the convenience store killings? His Honor the mayor has requested..." Pat gave Tom a wry smile. "Correction—demanded, an update for his press conference tomorrow."

"Nothing yet, sir. Can't be a coincidence that the same man owns the four stores involved. He's a target. We haven't been able to come up with a connection yet. I've checked out the family, especially the son and his acquaintances, but nothing gels so far."

I'd rather run this by Tom first, but here goes. Tentative but game, Kay raised her hand.

Pat's eyes lit on Kay. "Detective, anything to add?" He actually smiled instead of scowling at her, a confidence booster.

"I looked at the file on Friday. It nagged me all weekend long. I spoke to my teenage daughter and a few of her friends on Saturday. What they told me was a real eye-opener. Girls are apparently initiated into gangs the same way boys are. The initiation rites run the gamut: theft, breaking and entering, obtaining guns, and targeted hits. Makes me wonder how my kid knows this." Kay rolled her eyes. "The storeowner has a daughter. You should dig deeper into *her* activities and friends."

"Great job, Katie boy. Let's get on it right after the meeting." Tom grinned.

"Good catch, Sullivan...hmmm...Lynch." Patrick's eyes danced, his face flushed with apparent embarrassment at blurting out his first genuine, public compliment of her work.

Her heartbeat accelerated, elated, victorious. *Finally, Pat, I'm on your team.*

"Thank you, Captain." Kay beamed at him. "I hope it leads to solving the case."

Pat turned his attention to his checklist again. "Any questions before I turn the meeting over?"

He paused a couple seconds. When no one voiced a question, Pat remarked, "Okay, then. Captain Dowd wants a minute of your time."

He's here? Kay's skin prickled. Flynn unfolded his long, lean body from a folding chair at the far side of the room. Her heart fluttered as she observed his athletic gait, the flex of his biceps as he leaned on the lectern.

"I won't take up much of your time. Honestly, I don't even know if I have a case," Flynn admitted. "I understand you're all overworked. That's why I offered to open a file for your captain. Two sidewalk Santas died on the street recently from heart failure, according to the death certificates. Both were St. Nicholas Society to End Hunger volunteers who annually played Santa at outdoor locations around the city. They collect money during the organization's Christmas fund drive."

He consulted a paper he had placed on the

lectern. "Both were active, healthy men in their seventies with no prior history of heart disease, according to one of the deceased's wives. I fielded a call yesterday from one wife, Mrs. Heller. She believes her husband was murdered and insisted that we open a criminal investigation. She stated that Mr. Heller passed a full-body physical two weeks ago, purportedly in perfect health. I'm not sure where this will lead, but I could use a volunteer to do some of the legwork for me."

Pick me, Flynn. Nonchalantly, Kay raised her hand, and out of the corner of her eye, glimpsed two female officers eagerly raise theirs. *Shit, they're even waving their arms. Hmm, competition. Uh-uh, ladies. He's all mine.*

Flynn regarded Kay, apparently ignoring the other volunteer wannabes, and gave her a slow, compelling smile. Kay's vision narrowed as if no one else in the room, in the world, existed but Flynn.

"Detective Lynch, thank you for volunteering," Flynn stated.

The other potential volunteers' hands flopped into their laps.

"When you have a few moments, please come see me so we can go over the case file together," he concluded.

Resisting the urge to expel a satisfied sigh, Kay smiled pleasantly. "I'll report to your office as soon as I can, after I meet with Detective Gable, Captain Dowd."

Pat returned to the front of the room, and stood next to Flynn. "Anything else to discuss?" He scanned the room. "No? Let's get back to work. Dismissed. Stay safe."

****

Flynn's chair creaked as he sat behind his cluttered desk and perused his surroundings. Over a year on the job, and boxes he had toted in on his first day remained stacked in the corner. *If I analyzed my own behavior, I'd say I'm afraid to set down roots. Am I ready to start living again, rather than just surviving?*

Through his open office door, Flynn spied Kay bent over Gable's desk, her extremely diverting rear end visible between the cubicle's walls. He squinted for better focus, a fully absorbed, enthusiastic spectator. His chest tightened when she laughed at something Gable said.

The lady is enthralling. Her lingering, powerful effect continued to excite and vaguely puzzle Flynn. Objectively, Kay seemed the total opposite of any woman who had ever attracted him. His wife had been a tall, cool blonde—slow to smile and slow to warm. For the last few weeks, Kay's sunny grins, easy empathy and mesmerizing, soulful eyes had haunted his dreams, leaving him panting for her touch. *A petite, black-haired enchantress.*

As if she heard his thoughts, she stood up, turned in Flynn's direction and locked those bewitching blue eyes on his as she advanced toward his office. Clad in prim clothes, a white blouse tucked into gray slacks, and black leather flats, nothing about her attire could be tagged provocative. But the cut of her slim pants accentuated her figure: the flat stomach, the tantalizing movements of her thighs with each graceful step... He interpreted the gleam in Kay's lovely eyes, and her confident, erect carriage as her full knowledge of her own feminine wiles. A simple stroll across a squad room had the power to undo him.

Kay reached his door, a serene smile on her full, cherry-colored lips. His cell phone vibrated in his pocket.

Flynn jolted and dove his hand in his pocket to extract the phone. Glancing at the display, he waved Kay in, and then answered the call. "How's my girl today?"

"I'm happy because I'm talking to you, Flynn," Ma greeted him.

Kay's eyes narrowed, darkened, as she took a seat on the chair in front of his desk. His smile bloomed at the expression on her face. Was that jealousy that flashed in her eyes? *Sure is.*

He doubted that he haunted her dreams. *But she's attracted to me, too.*

"I just called to tell you I love you. And I miss you," Ma professed.

"I love you and miss you, too," Flynn responded.

Kay sniffed. Flynn's grin widened as he kept the phone pressed to his ear.

"I'll call same time next week," Ma promised.

"It's a date. Talk to you then." He disconnected the call and regarded Kay, curious if she'd question him about the caller.

"How about those Bears?" Kay asked.

Flynn furrowed his brows. "What?"

"The Bears. Didn't you watch the game yesterday?"

"Oh, football. No, I didn't. I worked yesterday," he responded. "Don't you want to know who was on the phone?"

Her shoulders shrugged slightly, a bemused expression on her face. "Why would I want to know that?"

I'm an idiot.

"The game was amazing," Kay related. "Such satisfaction, beating the Packers." She leaned back in the chair.

"You watch football?"

"I bleed blue and orange from August until February. Growing up in a house filled with boys, I had no choice. Join them or be left behind in the dust. I joined."

"My sisters watched chick flicks. I didn't mind

being left out." He chuckled, and then pointed to the cell phone on his desk.

"It was my mother. She calls me every Monday, like clockwork. My parents are staying in their house in Ireland for a couple of months, so she checks in and only talks for a few economical minutes." It was important to him to set things straight. He didn't want her to misunderstand, whether she cared or not. Flynn didn't play games with women. Until he'd met Kay, he hadn't considered any *play* with women since Bree died.

Kay's eyes warmed after his explanation, and her shoulders loosened. *Maybe she was just a touch jealous.*

"Wow, it's awesome they have a home in Ireland," she remarked. "I miss my parents so much when they go to Florida. In fact, they're back here for the holidays and staying with me. Even helped me to avoid another tongue-lashing from my brother. My other daughter has the same mysterious stomach ache her twin had, my first day on the job. I'm so relieved my mom enjoys taking charge with my kids when she's here. I can't imagine what it would be like if they were overseas for months."

"I noticed Pat treated you like one of the squad this morning. Have things gotten better between the two of you?"

"Seems so. Although Joe and Brian have avoided me since Halloween. Maybe Pat will have good things to tell them about my work." Her face lit with a smile. "Thank you again for covering for me when he was on the warpath. I owe you big time."

"A beautiful woman in my debt. Great way to start the week out."

Kay's head tilted demurely and her cheeks reddened.

Flynn enjoyed plying her with compliments. "Your single-handed takedown of Denny Irving is becoming legend." He laughed. "Sorry I didn't help."

"Hey, you supplied Connie's handcuffs." She chuckled.

"I'm very impressed with the way you've worked cases." *Gees, and how hot it was to see you in action.* "You've stirred up quite a buzz in the squad room."

"Good or bad buzz?" Frown lines creased on her brow.

"Only good," he assured her.

"I'm not doing anything special," she remarked, the jubilant glint in her eyes belying the modest declaration. "The value of a fresh eye for details."

"I certainly look forward to your opinion on this file." He pushed the folder across the desk. Kay opened it and settled back in the chair, one nicely shaped leg crossed daintily over the other.

Flynn studied her as she turned a page. His eyes strayed to the light tan spot on her shirt, instantly engrossed in the rise and fall of her breasts. His hands itched to reach out and slowly unbutton her blouse, release her breasts and explore the tender silk of her fair skin. He closed his eyes.

His lips trailed kisses down her milky neck. She tasted like honey warmed in the sun. He drew her closer as his mouth closed over her strawberry lips. His hand threaded through the coal black hair...

"Have you talked with St. Nicholas yet?

Flynn started and blinked his eyes open. "Huh?"

"I asked if you've talked to the St. Nicholas Society yet?"

"Um. No, I haven't."

"Have you responded to Mrs. Heller yet?"

"Who?"

"Mrs. Heller, the wife of the first deceased. Are you okay? You look feverish."

Flynn shook his head. "I'm fine. Sorry, I zoned out there for a minute. No, I haven't called her back."

"I'll start the phone calls. See if we can set up some interviews." Kay rose, the file held loosely in her hand. "Okay with you?"

"If you have the time, it's more than fine with me. I appreciate your help."

"This case interests me. I'm glad you accepted my offer."

Me, too. "I warn you, Mrs. Heller may be a loon." Flynn chuckled. "I hope she is. I dread trying to profile a Santa Claus killer."

Kay smiled. "That's why they pay you the big bucks, Captain. I'll let you know when the interviews are scheduled." Kay strode out of the office.

The sashay of her hips snagged his full concentration. *Damn, what a woman. She can take me down anytime.*

Chapter 6

Seated behind her desk again, Kay tackled her current caseload, energized by Pat's acknowledgment of her work at the morning meeting. The prospect of teaming with Flynn provided her additional motivation. *He called me a beautiful woman.* The compliment resonated with memories. Her husband, Mike, was the first and only man who had ever described Kay as beautiful, before.

Nearing lunch hour, Kay sacrificed food to work on Flynn's extra case. She opened the file, found the phone number, and dialed it. When the telephone recorder signal sounded, Kay said, "Mrs. Heller, this is Detective Kay Lynch, Chicago PD, following up…"

Clatter on the end of the line. "Hello…hello. Who is this?"

"Mrs. Heller?" Kay verified.

"Yes. I didn't catch your name," came her reedy, weak voice.

"I'm Detective Lynch. I understand you requested an investigation into the death of your husband?"

"Henry would do the same for me if somebody *killed* me," she asserted, her voice stronger, vehement. "And poor Gary Walton. I want you police to look into his death, too."

Kay sorted through the file and located copies of two death certificates. "Why is that?"

"He was killed just like my Henry," Mrs. Heller said. "I *told* you people. If you had listened, maybe he wouldn't have been murdered, too."

Kay slid a lined pad closer, clicked the end of a ballpoint a couple times. "Tell me why you believe your husband was murdered, ma'am."

"He was the strongest man ever. The doctor said he had the heart of a forty-year-old. He worked out, was proud of his body. He was *fine* when he left home. Two hours later he was *dead.*"

Kay looked closer at the death certificates indicating SCA, sudden cardiac arrest, as cause of death for both men. Those two documents and Flynn's notes comprised the contents of the file. *No autopsy reports?*

"Mrs. Heller, who conducted the autopsy?"

Soft sobs. She sniffled, took a few raspy breaths. "The city coroner, I think." The woman's voice wavered. "I didn't get a name. I can check the report for a signature. The tox panel showed nothing."

Kay registered mild surprise. "You obviously reviewed the report carefully."

"I'm a retired nurse. I know what I'm talking about."

"Mrs. Heller, did your husband have any enemies? Did someone threaten him?"

"Oh, no! Everybody loved him. He was the best Santa in the Society. Always drew a crowd."

Kay scribbled "witnesses" on the pad. "Ma'am, do you know who was present when your husband was...afflicted? I'd like to contact witnesses."

Ragged breathing through the earpiece. "No, I'm sorry." Dismay rang in her voice.

Lining out the word "witnesses" Kay drew a few rolling loops on the pad. "I don't know how to help you, Mrs. Heller. It appears your husband died of natural causes."

"I don't know who would hurt him! But *somebody* did." She halted.

Kay listened to white air as if the woman held her breath.

Then Mrs. Heller emitted a soft gulp or a hiccup. She whispered, "Don't think I'm crazy."

A couple more seconds of white air in Kay's ear before the woman continued, "Henry came to me in a dream and told me that I had to catch his killer."

Despite the far-out pronouncement, Kay's intuition fired. *I'm going to investigate this somehow.*

"I don't have any more questions for you right now, Mrs. Heller," Kay stated. "But I will look into this further and keep you informed."

A whoosh sounded, Mrs. Heller's deep sigh. "Thank you," she said.

Kay wrote "St. Nicholas Society" on her pad and underlined it twice while she dialed Flynn's extension on the intercom line.

"Dowd," he said.

"Flynn, this is Kay," she responded. "Can I update you on the, uh, Santa case?"

He laughed. "How about we talk over dinner? Do you have time after work for a quick bite at The Jury Box?"

Pleasure warmed her. "Sure. I'll stop by your office when I'm done today."

"Great," he said, his deep voice resonating in her ear. "See you then."

****

This is not a date. A quick bite to discuss a case is business. Period. Kay dashed across the street at Flynn's side and jumped the curb as the indicator "hand" glowed solid red. Brushing past Flynn as he held the door open, Kay's stomach dove, a swell of physical desire that sizzled through her body and set her limbs tingling.

Dead Santas the farthest thing from her mind, Kay scooted into her side of a booth for two in the noisy restaurant. Several uniforms bellied up to the bar, swilling beer and cracking peanuts out of their shells. A cluster of men bantered around the dartboard and heckled the shooter. Laughter, guffaws, and the din of conversations echoed in her ears. Leaning forward toward Flynn to avoid yelling, Kay said, "I told my mom I'd be an hour or so late getting home. Will that allow enough time to review the case, do you think?"

"Sure," Flynn replied. His warm breath smelled sweet, minty. "Whatever time you can spare on this." He picked up the two menus propped behind a catsup bottle and handed her one. "Is this inconveniencing your mother? We can meet tomorrow during the work day, instead."

This is definitely not social. "Not at all." Kay smiled at him. "Handling four kids is my mother's specialty."

"Okay, then." Flynn lowered his eyes and perused the menu.

Kay's attention lingered on Flynn's long fringe of black eyelashes that softened his rugged high cheekbones. When he cast a glance at her, she lowered her eyes rapidly, the print on the menu a blur.

"What are you in the mood for?" he asked as the waitress approached the booth.

Nothing we can do in The Jury Box. "Gooey ribs and fries." Kay slid her menu behind the bottle. "How about you?"

"Ribs for two," he told the waitress.

His menu joined hers as the waitress walked away. "So..." His green eyes shimmered in the dim light, and a warm smile parted his lips. Preoccupied with musing about tasting his lips, Kay half heard him say, "Let's hear your update on this weird case. Do we have a case at all?"

His eyes locked on hers, keen, interested. Shifting from fantasy to the reality of his interest in her, Kay reluctantly concentrated on his superior rank and the business at hand. "I interviewed Mrs.

Heller by phone today. She's adamant that her husband, Santa number one, was murdered and that Gary Walton's recent death corroborates her position. Walton is the other Santa volunteer."

Flynn shrugged. "Two sudden fatal heart attacks in elderly men out in the cold, swinging heavy bells, doesn't spell murder victims to me. Is this woman rational?"

"Well..." Kay paused as the waitress placed an oval platter of glistening barbecued ribs and heaps of fries in front of each of them.

The waitress left after supplying them with several packets of hand wipes. Flynn sliced a rib from the rack with his knife, and Kay continued, "The wife insists that the deceased visited her in a dream and charged her with finding his killer."

"I knew it." Flynn mouthed the rib bone, renewing Kay's fascination with his lips. "She's a loon."

Kay picked up her knife and sawed off a rib daintily. "Could be. But she struck a chord with me. Two men who worked for the same organization die of cardiac arrest on the job within a week of each other? Could that be a coincidence? Can't hurt to investigate it further. Right?"

Thick piquant sauce coated Kay's tongue as she bit into a rib.

Flynn chewed, swallowed. "What do you propose?"

"I want to talk to the ME and review the autopsy report or reports. I don't know if Gary Walton's body was autopsied. Also, I want to question the head of the St. Nicholas Society to End Hunger. See if I can glean enough to warrant a subpoena of personnel records."

"All right," Flynn agreed, and then his attention seemingly riveted to her lips as she innocently licked sauce off her finger.

Kay's heart somersaulted when he raised his eyes, his expression laden with frank desire. Infused with a sense of female power that he obviously thought her provocative, she smiled broadly. Her tone neutral, still all business, Kay said, "Want to come with me?"

A rib in his hand froze halfway on the trip from the plate to Flynn's mouth and he arched an eyebrow. "*What?*"

Hilarity bubbled inside Kay at his perception of her inadvertent "bedroom" double entendre. *Unless I meant it subconsciously.* "To the St. Nicholas Society," Kay clarified, straight-faced.

Flynn's low voice in answer was lost to Kay with the sudden outburst nearby of, "Pay up, loser!"

Boisterous snickers and exclamations ensued.

Laughing, Kay vamped up her volume and inquired, "What did you say?"

"I asked," Flynn's eyes held hers, "would you like to go to my apartment?"

"Oh." Confused, Kay probed, "To talk about the case?" She dragged her purse into her lap to rummage through it for her phone. "Okay. I'll call home and tell them I have to work late."

"No." Flynn's suggestive stare raised goose bumps on Kay's arms. "That wouldn't be accurate."

The phone loosely held in her hand, Kay stared back at him, silent, in rapt anticipation. When he didn't clarify further, she asked, "What shall I say to Mom?"

His eyes flashed, a dangerous beckoning, and he gave her a slow smile. "That you accepted an invitation for a...date."

"I see." Her heart drummed, a thudding in her ears. "I," she fumbled, attempting to construct a coherent sentence.

Leaning a breath away from her, he stated in a low voice, "I want you, Kay."

Pulse racing now, she whispered, "I want you, too. I don't play games, Flynn." She narrowed her eyes.

"Neither do I." He clasped her hand and she thrilled at the fiery sensation his touch invoked, eager to discover what he'd awaken in her if she allowed his hands to explore freely.

"I'll make that call now." The phone still hung loosely in her hand.

"I'll get the check." His eyes left hers in search of the waitress, but the heat from his unnerving, penetrating stare seconds before still enveloped her.

Shaky, Kay's fingers trembled as she dialed the phone.

Chapter 7

Kay followed Flynn's black sedan into the parking lot adjacent to his building, a vintage hi-rise bordering Lincoln Park. He steered into a space marked RESERVED in white spray-paint, and she noticed his pointing to an unpainted, empty spot deeper in the lot. She jerked her SUV into the tight space and sat, paralyzed, while the engine purred and her mind battled conflicting desires. *What am I doing here? I can change my mind. Pull out. Go home. Home, where it's safe.*

She tapped the ignition button and silenced the motor. Flynn left his car and bounded toward her. *Home, where I am lonely. I don't want to be lonely anymore.* The lights in the lot highlighted his face, his broad smile. *I want Flynn.*

Kay popped her seatbelt and pushed the car door open. *There is no place I would rather be tonight.*

Flynn's fingers curled around her hand as he clasped it to his side and led her through the glass door toward the security desk.

"Good evening, Mr. Dowd," the female guard greeted him. Her eyes bored into Kay. *Jealous are we? I don't blame you.* Kay smirked and squeezed Flynn's hand tighter.

"Hey, Sue," Flynn greeted the guard. "Have a great evening." He hurried to the elevator, his warm hand linked to hers.

Neither spoke as the elevator rose to the top floor.

Kay's nerves kicked in as the doors swished

open. "This is a nice building." Her voice trembled.

"It's not bad. Nice and clean and quiet. No noisy neighbors. Serves my purpose." He turned the key in the lock on his front door.

"Do you rent?"

"No. I own it. Well, the bank and I." He chuckled as he opened the door, let Kay pass and then followed behind her, snapping on the lights. "Welcome," Flynn said.

"Wow this is....well, this is unexpected."

He raised his eyebrows.

"I've seen your office," Kay joked.

He laughed as he took her jacket. "I guess this *is* a bit different. Would you like a glass of wine?"

"That sounds perfect."

He hung her jacket on a coat tree in the corner of the entryway and then entered the kitchen area.

Kay wandered around the living room, touching framed pictures and artfully placed bric-a-brac, her curiosity a pleasant distraction from her anxiety about being on a...date with Flynn.

"Red or white?" he called from behind the counter that divided the kitchen and living area.

She turned to face him. Four high wooden stools lined the counter, her view of Flynn's torso sectioned by the chairs' back rungs.

Nervous flutters churned in Kay's stomach. "Whatever you have is fine with me." *As long as it contains alcohol.*

"Okay. Make yourself at home." His hand rooted around in a cabinet drawer.

Kay resumed inspecting the room, her hands on her hips to curb their trembling. She surveyed the décor, determined to focus on her surroundings rather than what might come next.

A huge chocolate-brown corduroy couch, piled with rust and tan throw pillows, occupied a large part of the roomy area, and a well-worn, brown leather "man chair" abutted the sofa. Both pieces of furniture angled toward a mammoth flat-screen television that covered an entire wall. Taupe wood shutters, slats closed, dressed the windows.

She stepped over to the couch and fingered the orange-and-beige-striped afghan.

"Pretty," Kay remarked, admiring the artistry and soft texture of the woolen piece. "This looks homemade." She glanced at him.

Flynn leaned over the counter opening a bottle of wine. "It is." He twisted the cork off the opener.

Extracting glasses from an overheard cabinet, he placed them on the counter. "My mother crocheted it," he said.

"It's beautiful. I'm impressed. In general..." She smiled. "You've done a wonderful job decorating this room."

"As much as I would like to impress you, I can't take credit for all the pillows and doodads. The accolades go to MDO Design."

"You hired an interior decorator? I've heard of them," Kay commented.

"MDO are my sister's initials. Maeve Dowd O'Donnell owns the company." Flynn skirted the counter and closed the distance between them, carrying two glasses of ruby-red wine.

"Lucky you. Your sister has wonderful taste. And a pretty name. Maeve, queen of the fairies in Ireland." She grinned up at him, accepting the glass he offered. "I love this room."

"I'll pass on the compliment to Maeve." He raised his glass, clinked it against hers. "The place pales compared to you."

He sipped wine, his green eyes smoky over the rim of the glass, riveted on her.

Magnetized by his appreciative gaze, Kay drank too, the smooth fruity wine on her tongue, dizzy warm sensations cascading through her. She swallowed, cheeks flaming as she broke his stare. Polarized by uncertainty, her pulse raced. *Run out the door. Run into his bedroom and pray he follows.* Her eyes flitted around the room.

An oil painting hung between two windows anchored her attention amid the storm of indecision his nearness provoked. Brush strokes of vivid colors on the canvas imparted a three-dimensional quality to the image of a tree. Deep orange and maroon leaves mingled with pale and emerald greens, dotted with sunshine yellow as if the foliage were about to fall in the breeze.

The tiny brown F painted in the lower right corner prompted her to focus on his face again. "Flynn, did you paint this?"

He tilted his head, eyed the painting and replied, "Guilty."

"My God, Flynn, this is amazing. I didn't know you're an artist." Kay handed him her glass, hurried toward the windows, and planted herself directly in front of his artwork.

Flynn came up behind her and encircled her shoulders with his arms. "Was an artist." He nuzzled the nape of her neck. "A million years ago I thought I could make a living with a paintbrush. A wife and a little boy changed my mind."

Kay leaned back against his chest. Her heart pounded against her ribs.

Flynn swiveled around, rotating Kay a half circle within his embrace. "Ready for some more wine?"

Kay stared at the two wine glasses atop the coffee table in front of her. His strong fingers kneaded her collarbone, then dipped gently beneath the opening of her blouse and roamed under the topmost fringes of lace on her bra. Her stomach muscles clenched, her limbs loosened with a swell of desire.

She turned in his arms. "Honestly, no. I'm ready for you." Cupping his face with her hands, she drew his lips down to hers. The soft, tender kiss grew forceful, demanding, robbing her of breath. Kay's eyes remained closed when their lips parted.

His gentle tug on her hand nudged her into motion and she popped her eyes open. Flynn guided her down a hallway and through a doorway. His bedroom was illuminated when he flicked a wall switch.

This room surprised Kay. While his living room radiated hominess and warmth, his unwelcoming, stark bedroom held no trace of his sister's soft touch. A black armoire, a king-sized bed and a small end table added up to the only furnishings. An icy gray comforter covered the bed. No extra pillows, or doodads, as Flynn had called them, adorned the room.

Flynn released her hand, opened the end table's drawer and positioned a tealight candle on the tabletop. A sulfurous odor wafted as he lit a match, tipped the wick into flame and snuffed the match with a finger pinch. Retreating a couple steps toward the door, Flynn flipped the light off. Pale candlelight flickered. Another oil painting hung over his bed. Muted gray swirls surrounded the figure of a raven-haired woman standing in the center of the canvas. Spiky short hair framed her face, the features concealed in shadows. Kay brushed a hand through her own similar hairdo, noticing that 'F' had signed this painting, also.

"Another. It's interesting..." Kay sighed, delighting in his artistic skill. She sucked in a breath when he opened a button on her blouse. Delighting far more in this very different skill as his fingers grazed her cleavage, triggering a blast of longing.

"Yes. She's *very* interesting to me..." He kissed

the exposed skin on her neck, opened the next button.

"Is she your wife?" Kay asked, her voice husky, eyes closed now while his lips descended the succession of open buttons, rills of pleasure coursing through her.

"No. Bree was a Nordic blonde."

Her blouse gaping open, she shivered, quaked as his lips covered hers. The kiss ended on a whisper, "I titled the painting *Destiny*, long before I met my wife."

Kay opened her eyes, peered at his face.

His eyes mirrored the flickering candle. "Some things are meant to be." He lowered his head and kissed her breathless.

The kiss ended leaving Kay wanting him urgently, *now*. Her fingers trembled on the top button of his shirt.

Flynn clasped her hands to his chest, then raised them slowly and kissed her fingers. "Are you sure, Kay? We can...just have some wine. If we go much further I might not be able to stop."

His sea-green eyes twinkled in the candlelight. Kay unbuttoned his shirt in answer—her fingers steady now, her eyes unwavering on his. *I don't want you to stop.*

Shrugging her shoulders back, her blouse slid down her arms and fluttered to a landing on the dark gray rug. Dragging his shirt over muscled arms, she tossed it atop her blouse moments later. Flynn tugged his white T-shirt over his head, dropped it on the floor and unclasped Kay's bra with a swift, one-handed maneuver behind her back.

Cool air raised goose bumps on her feverish body and tightened her nipples, a sensation that tugged deep in her core. Yearning for contact, she moved closer and pressed her breasts against him, the soft down of chest hair contrasting with the muscled ridges of his torso against her skin. His hand slid to the band of her slacks, loosening it around her waist as he opened the button and grasped the zipper pull.

Self-conscious panic stabbed her and Kay shot her hand over his, jerking it stationary against her upper abdomen. "No," she blurted.

Raising her eyes to his, she read the confusion in the furrow of his brow. "I've had four children."

Flynn tilted his head, kindness glowing in his eyes. "Honey. Being a mother only makes your body more beautiful." He knelt and kissed her waist as he unzipped her pants and tenderly slid them down her legs. His warm hands cupped her hips and slid down along her thighs, drawing her panties with them.

Flynn laid his head against the softness of her belly, kissed the puckered flesh around the C-section scar that no amount of sit-ups had flattened. "You are incredibly beautiful," he said, his fingers brushing, probing between her legs.

Exquisite sensations rocked Kay. She moaned softly and squeezed his shoulders for balance against the piercing pleasure he stirred with his fingers and mouth. Tensing, neck arched, Kay surrendered to the gathering at her core until release crested and mushroomed, burst inside her like a wondrous explosion.

Gazing down at him, she uttered, "I can't... catch my breath..."

His cheeks creased with a sly smile. Bending his head, Flynn trailed kisses up along her body as he stood, lifted her off her feet and placed her in the center of the bed. Propped over her, his lips consumed her mouth, hungry, insistent. His hand caressed her body in sweeping arcs, soft, firmly kneading, and then featherlight, driving her wild with desire.

"Please..." Her breath came in pants. "I *need* you inside me. *Now*. Hurry and get protection."

His hand froze in place on her shoulder. "I don't have anything," he replied thickly.

"That's not funny." She opened her eyes, head spinning and caught his chagrined expression. "You really don't?"

"I'm sorry. I didn't plan on..." He flopped flat on his back next to her.

Staring at the ceiling a few seconds, she crossed her arms over her breasts, suddenly chilled. "I feel like I'm sixteen, making out on the couch and my parents just opened the back door."

Kay giggled.

Flynn snickered.

Hilarity escalated, contagious, until their boisterous laughter rocked the bed.

Tears streaming, Kay exclaimed, "I can't catch my breath." She propped up on one elbow surveying his face.

He blew a breath through pursed lips, exasperated. "Leaving you breathless like this...isn't what I had in mind."

"Hmm." Eyes locked on his, Kay undid his belt and unzipped his pants. Slipping her hand under the elastic waistband of his briefs, she caressed him.

"Lord." He exhaled, his eyelids lowered.

Stroking him first with languid movements, then more aggressively, Kay's pleasure increased as she pleasured him. Thrilled that he cried out, "Kay!" as he came, she rolled onto her back, satisfied, if not sated.

She lay on her side, head resting on Flynn's bare, solid chest. With each steady rise and fall of his breathing, soft black chest hairs tickled the side of her cheek. Tucking the comforter over her, she sighed.

"I'm sorry," Flynn said.

"Sorry? You don't have anything to be sorry about."

"I promise next time I'll have a drawer filled with protection. That's if you'll give me a second chance?"

A drawer full? Kay smiled, snuggled closer to him. "Absolutely."

His finger tipped beneath her chin and he kissed her, his lips soft, a faint tang of sweet barbecue sauce on his tongue.

When his lips left hers Kay's mind strayed toward thoughts of home. *Is schoolwork done? Did they pitch in and help Mom with chores?* Nestled warm in his arms, still aching for more of him, Kay wanted to ignore the call to motherhood a while longer, but couldn't. "I better get going."

Sitting up in bed, she made a grab for the comforter and draped it in front of her chest, irrationally awkward about nudity.

Flynn's abs tensed as he sat, swung his legs over the side of the bed and stooped to sweep his undershirt and shirt off the floor. He stood, shirts in one hand, regarding Kay. His fly open, glimpses of white briefs riding the etched V of his lower abdomen tempted her to fling the comforter off and give him that second chance right now.

"I'll wait in the living room," Flynn said.

"Thanks," Kay replied.

He turned away and strode out the door, the rear view every bit as tantalizing as the front. Kay shivered as she hopped off the bed and retrieved her clothes scattered on the floor. She dressed quickly and hurried out of the room.

Flynn re-corked the wine bottle on the kitchen counter and zipped up his leather jacket.

"Going somewhere?" Kay approached him.

"I'll follow you home." He held up her coat by the shoulder seams, the lining toward her.

Kay slid one arm into a coat sleeve, then the other arm, while retorting, "That's crazy. I live a half hour away. I'm a cop, too."

Buttoning her coat, she faced Flynn. "I don't need protection."

His eyes widened and he grinned. "Saves me a trip to the drugstore."

She snorted and rolled her eyes with a shake of her head.

Flynn cupped a hand around her shoulder. "When I take a lady out on a date, I make sure she gets home safely."

Kay bumped her hip against his. "Don't be silly..."

Flynn held his hand up. "I take care of my lady. Get used to it."

His lady. I like the sound of that. "Just so you know you don't have to."

"I want to. Let's go."

Outside in the parking lot, hands linked, Flynn escorted Kay to her car. At the driver door, he threaded his hands through her hair, drew her mouth toward his and kissed her deeply before he said, "Thank you for a wonderful evening."

Giving him a dreamy smile, Kay responded, "Thank you. See you tomorrow at work."

She slid into her seat when Flynn opened the door, fired the ignition and reversed out of the space, waiting at the lot exit for Flynn to pull in behind her. He flashed his lights and she proceeded to drive toward home.

Tears stung the corners of Kay's eyes.

He's very special, Mike, a good guy. You'd like him. With what we shared during our marriage, God knows I'm horny...I'll never forget you, honey, I promise. I'll always miss you, but I'm ready now, my love. I know you would want me to be happy. I think Flynn can make me happy. I will always love you, my darling.

The tears brimmed and rolled down her cheeks.

****

When she reached the mouth of her driveway, Kay triggered the electric garage door opener, acknowledged Flynn's headlights flash with a wave of her hand, and drove up the concrete drive into the garage. After turning off the overhead light, she peeked out the garage window. Flynn executed a three-point turn out on the street. His face illuminated fully as he lit a cigarette, and then only the contours of his head facing her were visible as he sat and apparently stared at her house several minutes before he drove away. Kay remained at the window until his taillights disappeared.

Destiny? Yes. I could get very used to your protection.

****

Jingle bells, Santa smells.
You deserve to die.
Mix the drink,
God you stink!
Ho, ho, ho. Good-bye.

A package of dental floss clatters into the red plastic shopping basket hooked over my arm while I glance sideways at the happenings outside.

A woman rushes into the revolving door, shoves a half circle around and pokes her head into the store. "Call an ambulance! Call an ambulance, Santa collapsed."

The woman's shrill voice echoes in the drugstore and hurts my ears. What a drama queen. The clerk's hands shake as he punches the digits on his cell phone. My concerned face reflects in the mirror behind the counter.

Damn, I am good, and you said I wasn't good at anything, Father. Proving you wrong once again, aren't I?

"I'll be right with you," the clerk says as he, too, rushes outside.

Pocketing the dental floss, I return the basket to the stack near the door and hurry outside to join the gathering crowd of hovering do-gooders. Patting my pocket, I smile. You can always use dental floss.

Chapter 8

Ten pies is probably overkill. Hell, I'll bet Kay will bring a dozen—home baked. Flynn stowed three shopping bags loaded with bakery boxes in the back seat of his car, shut the door, and depressed the button on the electronic locking device. A chirp sounded from the car as he paced briskly back into his building, his boots scuffing the pavement and pulverizing brittle leaves in his wake.

He hadn't seen Kay the past few days, their duty shifts apparently out of sync. The fact had left him discontented, hungry for contact with her, and conflicted about the best way to plan another private evening that ended better. Vaguely embarrassed and hugely frustrated, Flynn remained hopeful that she'd overlook his tarnishing their first intimate time together with lack of—foresight.

No doubt today wouldn't offer any opportunity for intimacy. Flynn wondered if Kay knew that Pat had extended a casual invitation for him to join the family for Thanksgiving dinner at his house. *Should I have checked with her first before accepting? I'll probably meet her kids. Is she ready for that? Am I?*

Acting on the impulse that had occurred to him while loading the car, Flynn descended to the basement on the elevator. At the end of the narrow hallway lined with storage cages, he turned the key, unhooked the padlock, and swung open the chain-link gate on his designated area. He surveyed the clutter of boxes and canvases. *Looks better than my office.* Stooping to sort through his paintings, Flynn selected one and stood, blowing dust off the top edge.

Destiny II. The second in the panel of four he had created for a gallery show, seemingly eons ago, featured the same coal-black-haired woman's image in the foreground. Her facial features blurred except for a radiant smile, and the background strokes of lighter grays and browns than the first painting Kay had noticed blended toward the far horizon. A shimmering, pastel-yellow focal point along the horizon backlit the woman's figure.

Flynn had sold the other two paintings in the series at the show—in the third, a noonday sun shone on the indistinct face of the woman; the fourth depiction bathed her in moonlight. He stared at the woman's smile, contagious, more dazzling than the sunrise behind her. *Kay.*

Tucking the canvas under his arm, he locked the storage cage and ambled down the hall to the elevator. He'd give Kay the painting, perhaps today. Convinced it was meant to be hers, he mulled over his equal conviction that she was meant to be his on the way back out to his car.

Behind the wheel, bound for the stationhouse, guilt pinched him at the thought of Bree. When they were newlyweds, Bree had detested Flynn's aspirations to be a full-time artist and had never admired his paintings. For the sake of harmony, Flynn had stopped painting and had focused on his then-regular job as a low-ranking police officer. To further appease his wife and fulfill her ambitions for him, he somehow squeezed in completion of a graduate course in psychology, since criminal profiling had interested him. No sacrifice involved, Flynn had discovered he loved everything about law enforcement.

And then Bree had decided that she detested police work. Their rocky marriage had begun the downward slide toward divorce when a last ditch effort at reconciliation resulted in Flynnie's conception. Flynn had buried his resentment under workaholic dedication, all the while dreading the life sentence that the baby's impending birth represented.

Stunned by his elation when he held Flynnie in his arms that first time, Flynn's entire world had transformed with his son's miraculous presence. Flynnie had loved the way his father loved him, unlike his wife, and had extracted uncharacteristic warmth from Bree. In truth, she was a good mother, forgiven for her increasing coldness toward Flynn for that simple fact.

Flynn rolled into the lot adjacent to the precinct and left the car. Moving on autopilot, he mechanically plodded across the pavement into the building, his senses dulled by reverie. He didn't miss Bree. At least not with the gnawing, ever-present pain that missing Flynnie entailed.

He reached his office, switched on the lights, swung around the desk, and sat in his chair. *I miss Kay.* Flynn let the admission sink in—waited for a pang of conscience or guilt for not grieving the loss of his wife enough, but none came. Kay spurred an optimism and zest for life in him that he'd never experienced with any woman. On this day of Thanksgiving, he would be grateful for that.

His intercom buzzed and he answered, "Dowd."

"Captain Dowd, a caller is asking for either you or Detective Lynch. Will you take the call?"

"Sure, put it through." Receiver to his ear, when the call transfer connected with a click Flynn announced, "Captain Flynn Dowd."

"Captain, my name is Sandra Walker. I'm the managing director of the St. Nicholas Society to End Hunger."

"Yes, ma'am. What can I do for you?"

"Sir, one of our volunteers was just pronounced dead at his post outside the CVS pharmacy on West

Washington. I'm devastated about this..."

Flynn's senses sharpened. "How did you know to contact me?" he probed.

"We've had two other volunteers die recently, Henry Heller and Gary Walton. I thought it was an awful coincidence until Henry's wife, Bonnie, informed me that she had called the police to investigate her husband's death."

Opening his desk drawer, he pulled the "Santa" file. "That's correct. Have you been in contact with Mrs. Heller today?"

"Yes, right after the store manager reported Cy Bailey's collapse about a half hour ago. I asked Bonnie Heller for your number. She's right. This can't be a coincidence. I don't know what to *do* about this."

"You did the right thing, Ms. Walker. Where did they take the body?" Flynn opened the file, flattening it on his desk. He jotted the director's name on the inside of the folder, noted the caller ID read-out, and added her telephone number next to her name.

"To the Cook County morgue."

"Thank you. I'll look into this right away. Are you available to speak with me, perhaps later today?"

"Uh..."she hesitated.

It's Thanksgiving. "That may not be necessary, ma'am. I realize it's a holiday."

"Oh, thank you, Captain. I'm actually calling from home. I have a houseful of company coming in about an hour."

"I'll call you tomorrow to arrange a time to meet. Have a nice Thanksgiving."

"You, too, sir. Thank you very much."

Flynn disconnected the call and depressed the intercom button. "Lucas," came the response.

"Hey, Josh. Can you get Kay Lynch on the line

for me?"

"Sure. Hang up and I'll ring you back."

"Thanks." Flynn complied and then gazed out the window at the low ridge of gray clouds threatening snow until the anticipated call came through.

Flynn cut off the first ring with a quick punch to the line button. "Flynn Dowd."

"Happy Thanksgiving, Flynn. What's up?"

Gratified by the sweet lilt in Kay's voice, Flynn responded, "First, Happy Thanksgiving, Kay. Next, we have another suddenly deceased Santa Claus."

"*Whoa.* Okay. How do I help?"

"Meet me at Cook County morgue as soon as you can?"

A racket sounded, a high-pitched squeal.

"Pipe down!" Kay yelled, thankfully away from the mouthpiece or he'd have needed a new ear. "Give me about forty-five minutes, and I'll be there."

"I'll hop a cab and will probably beat you there. The deceased's name is Cy Bailey. See you later."

****

Flynn patted his jacket over the shoulder holster's bulge as he entered the building. Unnecessary to pack a gun for a visit to the morgue, but he had made it a daily practice since Kay had taken down Denny while Flynn functioned as a bystander.

Antiseptic aromas permeated the air inside. It had been a long time since Flynn had seen active duty, inhaled the smell of sterilized death. Even the layout of this place was foreign to him. He roamed down a labyrinth of hallways until he found an occupied office.

The plump, white-haired woman clad in lavender sweats and an incongruous pearl choker sat behind the desk. She glanced up over Ben Franklin bifocals at his rap on the door. "Uh-huh..."

she lengthened the last syllable on a Southern drawl and let it hang there while she stared at him with brown eyes, glassy with boredom.

"Is the end of your sentence 'you pain in the ass'?" Flynn challenged her.

"You said it, sugar, I didn't." She still regarded him with that bored expression. "Want to substitute a name for 'pain in the ass'?" Then she smiled broadly, apparently amused.

"Flynn Dowd, Captain under Patrick Sullivan's command, area 1," he stated smiling widely. Flynn stepped toward her desk, right hand extended.

"Cecilia Martin, City Medical Examiner." Still smiling graciously, she gave his hand one dainty shake and then withdrew her hand.

"I think I like you, Ms. Martin."

"You can use my first name, Flynn. What's not to love?" Her eyes twinkled. "I take it you're here on a case."

"That's right. I want to talk about Cy Bailey, possible homicide victim. Brought in about an hour ago. COD? What can you tell me after examining his body?"

Cecilia swiveled her rolling desk chair in position to use a computer keyboard, her face in profile. With creamy unlined skin and cheeks a pretty pink, she was a very attractive woman, maybe in her mid to late sixties. *Must have been a knockout in her prime.*

Her fingers flew over the keys, a series of eight clicks and a tap on the enter button. Tilting her head far back to peer at the screen through the bifocals, her eyes tracked back and forth. "I haven't assigned him yet." She rode the chair back to face him. "Nothing to talk about."

Her eyes focused past him, her face lit with a huge smile. "Kay Sullivan?"

Kay stood in the hall outside the ME's office,

beaming a smile at Cecilia. Clad in snug jeans and a white T-shirt beneath a black leather bomber jacket, Kay was trim, confident, and utterly irresistible to Flynn. "It's Lynch now. Mother of four and..." She frowned as her voice caught.

Cecilia's shoulder sagged. "Criminy, I knew that. I'm sorry. I sent a card when your husband passed. Did you get it?"

"I did, thank you." Kay smiled sweetly.

Cecilia's face brightened. "Land sakes, what have you done to your hair? You look just like some rock singer whose name escapes me..."

Kay rustled her spiky haircut. "You like it?"

"Love it. Come get a hug." She shoved her chair back and stood behind the desk, arms opened wide.

Kay bustled into the office, leaned over the desk, threw her arms around the woman and exclaimed, "Ceci, it's been ages."

'Ceci' squinted at Flynn over Kay's shoulder. "We go way back."

"I see," Flynn commented. "Kay is the detective working this case with me."

Kay straightened and turned toward him with a smile. "Hi, Flynn. What have I missed?"

"Not much..."

"I'm assigning Cy Bailey's autopsy," Cecilia interjected. "To me. Anything specific you want me to investigate, Kay?"

Kay pursed her lips and cast her eyes upward before she replied, "I suspect the cause of death is sudden cardiac arrest. We're pursuing a link with this death and two others, Henry Heller and Gary Walton. Same COD. All three were volunteer Santas for the St. Nicholas Society. Presume Cy Bailey was murdered. Check the body for possible injection punctures or toxins in the blood screen. I'm a blank page on this, but I do want to scrutinize the autopsy reports for the first two, also. See if I can find a common thread. Anything to add, Flynn?"

"You're doing fine," he responded.

Kay clasped her hands together and said, "Okay, Ceci. Can you start on this now?"

Cecilia rounded her desk and leaned a hip on the front edge. "I'm here for the next eight hours, so, yes. But you don't have to stick around. Surely you want to spend Thanksgiving with your kids?"

"I do, yes..." Kay hesitated. "But this comes first."

Cecilia stood circling an arm over Kay's shoulder. "I'll handle this as top priority. Tomorrow morning is soon enough. Let's say 6:30?"

Kay's face pinched, a shadow of regret in her blue eyes. "Okay. Thanks. I'll be here," she agreed.

"You're not on the duty roster tomorrow, Kay. All right with you, Cecilia, if I meet with you instead?"

"Are you sure?" Kay's eager expression amused him.

He smiled. "Yep." Flynn held out his right hand toward Cecilia and she accepted the handshake.

"Nice to meet you, Flynn."

"A pleasure, Cecilia. See you in the morning."

Despite the pungent odors in the morgue, Kay's perfume sweetened the air as he navigated the maze of hallways with her and exited the building.

"She's the best there is," Kay said. "We're lucky she's the ME on this."

"Good," Flynn replied. "If you're happy, I'm happy."

Outside, the brisk air invigorated Flynn, the overcast skies no longer a damper on his mood. Kay's presence had him lighthearted and aroused. *Happy*.

Halting on the driver's side of her SUV, he used the truck as a privacy shield and drew her into his arms. He kissed her soft lips, acutely aware of her leaning more heavily against him as she melted along with him in the heady connection. Reluctantly, he withdrew his lips from hers, one kiss never enough. "I'll see you later at Pat's house."

"*Really*? That's great." The enthusiasm in her voice and the delight gleaming in her upturned eyes gratified Flynn.

She scanned the parking lot. "Where's your car?"

"Back at the squad's lot. I came here in a cab."

Kay rested a hand on the door handle. "Want a lift back?" She bent her left arm and glanced at her watch. "I *think* I have enough time to fit in the drive back to my house and then out again to the city with the troops to make it to Pat's on time."

"Nah." Flynn pecked a kiss on her lips. "See you later. Don't rush."

With a parting grin, Kay opened her car door and ducked inside.

Chapter 9

"Hurry up! The bus is leaving," Kay yelled up the stairs. Drumming an impatient beat on the handrail, she waited to hear pounding feet. Nothing. "Come on! Turkey's getting cold!"

Mary appeared at the top of the landing. Tromping down the stairs, her blonde ponytail bobbing, she frowned when she reached her mother. "You look so pretty, Mom. Should I change into a dress, too?"

Kay glanced downward, inspecting her outfit, a long-sleeved knit dress with a hem at mid calf over high-heeled, knee-high boots. The clingy material accentuated her figure, made her feel feminine, maybe sexy. Had she not learned earlier that Flynn would be at Pat's, jeans and a sweater like Mary's would do.

"Oh, no. You look perfect." Kay lovingly touched the side of Mary's face, the baby soft skin luxurious beneath her hand. *My sweet girl.*

Three more "sweet" children pounded down the steps, her twins in matching *Hannah Montana* shirts over jeans, followed by Mike—also in jeans topped with a Notre Dame sweatshirt, iPod ear bud wires dangling like a stethoscope over his chest.

"Let's go," Kay suggested, on a bead toward the door leading to the garage.

"I want to wear a dress, too," Peggy whined.

"Me, too," Amanda echoed. "And boots, like you, Momma."

She faced her daughters. "We don't have time. You both look beautiful. First one to the car rides shotgun."

Kay turned around and advanced toward the door, expecting both girls to shoot past her. *Nope. Damn, why did I put on a dress?*

Once more, Kay faced the twins, identical pouts on their faces, obviously working up to whines. "Okay. Go put on the dresses you wore to Lila's birthday party."

Peggy pivoted and shot back upstairs. Amanda remained glued to the spot, a sour expression on her face. "I want to wear knee-hi boots, too."

"You don't own knee boots, Amanda."

"We can stop at Target on the way to Uncle Pat's." She widened her eyes, the charming supplicant. "*Please*, Momma."

Kay shook her head and smiled. "Nope. Five minutes to change if you still want to wear a dress. Scoot."

Amanda trudged upstairs as if she wore lead boots, defeated by Kay's final word, her sour puss a lingering rebellion.

The lack of traffic on the Eisenhower expressway compensated for minutes lost at home, and Kay preceded her family up to Pat's door, precisely at four o'clock, the invited time. Her children clustered around her, she shifted a bottle of wine into the crook of her left arm while a six-pack of beer dangled in her left hand, and rang the bell. A wreath of dried flowers hung on the row house's red door, a new addition since Kay had last visited Pat. *Charlie's touch, no doubt. I remember when I made wreaths like this for my entire neighborhood.*

Pat opened the door, enfolded Kay and then each of the kids in a bear hug, and showed them to the living room. Kay encountered standing-room-only conditions with the adults of the Sullivan family overloading the small space.

The kids milled around, greeted relatives, and

then scattered in search of their cousins or a quiet spot to watch TV, listen to music, or otherwise escape the adults.

The delectable smell of roasted turkey tantalized Kay. Especially delightful to her was the fact she hadn't lifted a finger to create the dinner she was about to enjoy.

Charlie, Pat's fiancée, bounded over to Kay and embraced her. "Quite a frenzy, huh? I must have been nuts to volunteer to cook today." She smiled, the gracious hostess, as Kay handed her the bottle of wine and carton of beer.

"I didn't have time to bake, so I brought this," Kay said.

"Thank you. Do you believe Flynn brought *ten* pies? We are set." Charlie hugged Kay.

Kay surveyed the faces in the living room and didn't find Flynn. "Where is..."

"Damn good thing *somebody* brought pies," Joe declared. "Sure as hell *you're* too busy to think of your family."

Bobbie, cradling baby Emma and seated next to Joe on the green leather sectional, poked her husband in the side of his arm with her free hand.

Kay glared at Joe. "Don't start," she commanded him.

"I'll put the beer in the fridge. Dinner's almost ready," Charlie commented, diplomatically. She proceeded down the hall toward the kitchen.

Obviously unperturbed by his wife's physical response to his sarcasm and Kay's threatening tone, Joe continued, "We all were looking forward to your baking, Kay. But I suppose now you don't have time for *tradition.*"

"Yeah," Brian chimed in.

"Oh for the love of Pete," Brian's wife Matty commented, her tone disgusted.

"Speak for yourself, Joe," Danny demanded.

"Mom?" Bobbie shifted on the couch. "Could you please take Emma upstairs to her travel bed?" She raised Emma upward in her arms, gazing at her mother-in-law. "Little ears," she concluded as explanation.

Jean Sullivan smiled as she rose from her chair, crossed the room and enfolded the infant in her arms. "Here we go, love," she cooed to the baby. "Nana will sing you a lullaby."

As Jean passed Kay, she pecked a kiss on her cheek. "Go get 'em," she whispered in her ear.

Kay brushed her mom's shoulder fondly and then strolled over to a seat on the folding chair her mother had vacated.

The sound of Mom's footfalls receded, and Bobbie confronted Joe, "Since when are you such a chauvinist? If I wanted to go back to the Agency would you be a total ass about it?"

Joe's face softened beneath his black eye patch as he regarded his wife. "That's different."

"How is it different?" Kay challenged.

"I get what Joe is saying," Brian defended his brother.

"You *do?*" Matty asked, aghast. "It doesn't make any sense at all."

"It's just different," Joe insisted. "You're my wife, not my sister." He stared at Bobbie, a glint in his blue eye. "I've seen you in action. You're amazing."

Kay's cheeks enflamed as her temper flared. "What a hypocrite! Are you implying that I don't know what I'm *doing on the job?*"

"I'm *stating* that you don't *belong* on the job," Joe declared.

"Exactly," Brian concurred.

"What the *hell?*" Kay blustered as Flynn strolled into the room.

Their eyes connected. A slow smile bloomed on

Flynn's face while Kay's cheeks burned. Sidetracked, some of her anger abated in the grip of the sexual attraction he evoked. The silence tangible, it seemed the whole family was attuned to the current that sizzled between her and Flynn. Afraid to give her brothers something else to poke at, she debated whether it was worth it to continue this argument in Flynn's presence. But Joe's reasoning was too incomprehensible to let it go. "I'm *good* at what I do. Tell him, Flynn."

Flynn made to speak, but closed his lips, flicking his eyes from face to face. With a nod of his head he said, "She brought down a man twice her size without ever pulling her weapon..." Flynn grinned at Kay, "...and essentially no backup. I'm partnering with her now on a case. She's analytical, methodical. She has great instincts. I trust her to have my back."

Flynn's arm casually draped over Kay's shoulder as he stood next to her chair.

Joe squinted his eye, stared at Flynn as if sizing him up. "I won't have my sister risking her life with you."

Kay sat speechless while protests from the women overlapped, "Shut up, Joe!"

"Don't listen to him, Kay!"

"Good Lord, what a stupid thing to say!"

Pat's authoritative voice sounded from the corner of the room where he stood leaning against the wall. "She's doing a good job."

Kay's mouth hung open. Victorious, she smiled at Pat, couldn't resist asking, "Can you say that *again?*"

Pat shoved away from the wall and strode toward the dining area crammed with rows of tables. His back to her, and the rest of the adult family members in the living room, Pat stated loud and clear, "She's doing a good job. I'm glad to have her on my squad."

Leaning over the banister, Pat hollered up the stairwell, "Come on, kids! Time to eat!"

As if a starter horn blared, her brothers and their wives were on their feet in motion toward the dining room. Kay rose from her seat and linked her hand into the crook of Flynn's arm, the heat of the family's attention on her palpable.

Daddy made slow progress from the kitchen into the dining room burdened by a huge, glistening, roast turkey on a platter that barely contained the bird. Drumsticks overlapping the plate's edges rested on the tablecloth when he set the platter down. He peered at his kids' faces as they approached him with keen interest. "Did I miss something?"

"Yeah..." Joe boomed out.

"I'll kill you if you say another word," Bobbie threatened between clenched teeth.

A stampede of feet sounded on the stairs. The cacophony of voices on the high-ceilinged first floor echoed. Kay supposed the adult generations of the family suffered at least low-grade headaches. *I sure have one.*

She dropped her hand from around Flynn's bicep as her kids drifted into the room. Wiggling her index finger, Kay beckoned them over. "This is Captain Flynn Dowd," she said. "He works with me and Uncle Pat. Flynn, this is Mike, Mary, Peggy and Amanda."

"Nice to meet you, Captain," Mike said, shaking Flynn's hand.

"A pleasure, Mike," Flynn replied.

Mike held a chair out for Kay, and she sat while she observed Flynn shake Mary's hand.

Mary sat next to Kay and Mike took his place on the other side of his mother.

Flynn fixed his attention on the twins. "I like your dresses," Flynn said. "You both look pretty as a picture."

"Thank you," Peggy chirped.

"Momma wouldn't buy me boots, though," Amanda groused.

Kay rolled her eyes at Flynn's questioning glance. He smiled and sat across from Kay. Mom strolled behind Flynn's chair, dandling Emma. With a glance at Bobbie, Jean seated the baby in a high chair next to Flynn and belted her in. "She wasn't the least bit sleepy," Jean explained to her daughter-in-law, who took the seat on the other side of the high chair.

The family in place, Mom directed, "Patrick, say grace, please."

At the head of one table, Pat linked hands with Charlie and his mother. "Bless this..."

"Da, da, da, da!" Emma jabbered.

"Aw, that's my girl," Joe, the proud "Da," announced.

Pat's eyes twinkled as he continued, "Bless this, oh, Lord, for these thy gifts that we are about to receive through thy bounty. Faster we eat, faster we watch football. Amen!"

Pat wielded a carving knife as bowls of vegetables, stuffing, and cranberries, and breadbaskets piled with biscuits, changed hands around the tables. Emma grabbed at Flynn's huge hand that he skittered back and forth across her high chair tray like a crazed tarantula. Her delighted belly laughs warmed Kay to her toes. She spooned mashed potatoes onto her plate and passed the bowl to Mary, attentive to Flynn's antics entertaining the baby.

He brushed Emma's nose with a gentle hand swipe and then poked his thumb between his index and middle finger. "Got your nose!" He displayed his thumb to the baby, his eyes wide, his mouth an O.

Emma's blue eyes saucers, Flynn tapped her

nose with his thumb. "I'll put it back," he declared. She giggled, and Bobbie offered her a teething biscuit. The baby gummed it, brownish drool pooling in the corners of a rosebud mouth.

Flynn winked at Kay and then focused on filling his plate. He ate, apparently oblivious of the gooey cookie Emma poked against his ear and of the swell of deep affection for him that must surely be shining in Kay's eyes.

From experience as a hostess for this bunch, Kay fancied she could read Charlie's thoughts when, minutes later, the men rose from the table for ritual football viewing. *Hours and hours of work, and dinner's over in less than fifteen minutes?*

Toting stacks of dishes and bowls containing meager remnants of food, the women gathered in the kitchen for ritualistic KP.

"That Flynn is a *stud*," Bobbie exclaimed as she plunged her hands into sudsy water in the sink.

"And did you see him with Emma?" Molly asked, an enraptured expression on her face. "Our girl's in love."

"It was too cute," Kay added, enfolding a wet plate in a dishtowel.

"I wasn't referring to Emma," Molly said, bumping her hip against Kay's.

"Uh," Kay stammered.

"Oh, don't you deny it," Bobbie chimed in. "Did you see that eye lock when Flynn caught sight of Kay? Geez. And the way he defended you against my idiot husband? Too sexy for words." Bobbie fanned her face with a hand, splattering water on the counter.

Kay's heart drummed, speechless. She couldn't wedge a word in, anyway.

Chuckling, Molly said, "I enjoyed just watching him walk into the room. *Hot*." She shivered.

"I'll probably have dreams about him tonight,"

Matty joked.

"Hell, yeah. Me, too," Bobbie agreed leering in Kay's direction.

"Oh," Charlie interjected, "And he's sweet, too. I talked with him while I prepared dinner. Did you know he lived in Ireland until he was eight? He turned on a brogue while he related that. I'm such a sucker for accents."

"So, Kay," Bobbie's eyes bored holes through her. "Anything you'd like to tell us?"

"Leave Kay alone," Mom demanded, a gleam in her eye. "She's entitled to her privacy...*but*..." Mom hesitated. "We are all interested in your happiness, dear."

My happiness. A lovely sensation fluttered inside. "Well," Kay began. "We had dinner the other night. And I..." Kay grinned at the women grinning at her like maniacs. "I *enjoyed* myself immensely."

They hooted as Mom said, "That's nice, dear. Maybe Daddy and I will stay until after Christmas." She handed Kay another wet plate to dry. "Just in case you need a babysitter."

Bobbie dried her hands on the sides of her jeans. "I'm going in there to root against whichever team Joe favors, just for fun."

"Me, too," Matty said. "I can't wait to chew Brian's ear off for giving you a hard time, Kay."

Kay smiled. "I'll help Mom and Charlie bring coffee and pie into the den. I...I love you guys."

****

Flynn stood. "Thanks, Pat and Charlie, for an excellent meal. Everybody," he surveyed the family gathered in the den, "thank you for including me today. Happy Thanksgiving."

"I'll walk you to the door," Kay offered, ignoring Joe's pointed glance in her direction.

Outside on the stoop, Kay faced Flynn, yearning to throw her arms around him and nestle against his chest. Full of thanksgiving, he had stolen her heart today, and she was jubilant at the loss.

His eyes warm, gazing down at her, Flynn said, "The porch light and the eyes of countless Sullivans are upon us." He chuckled. "Pretend I'm kissing you, for Lord knows, I want to."

"Same for me," Kay replied on a smile. "Safe home."

"I'll be in touch tomorrow after I meet with Cecilia Martin," he promised.

"Good." Kay squeezed his hand and turned back toward the door.

****

"Did you go home and sleep at all last night?" Flynn inquired when he encountered Cecilia, seated on a high stool in the autopsy room. Still clad in the same lavender sweatsuit as yesterday, bluish bags under her eyes, the ME appeared ragged, exhausted.

"No and yes," Cecilia answered. "My Zack brought the Thanksgiving meal to me." She smiled. "I slept on a cot in one of the empty offices for a couple hours. He's still sleeping on his matching cot. Don't know what I'd do without that man."

Flynn eyed the corpse prone on the table, intestines and organs in silver basins, a sea of stainless steel and fluorescent glare. "Cy Bailey, I presume."

"Affirmative," Cecilia quipped. "SCA. No arterial plaque to speak of. No contraction of the coronary arteries, yet massive heart muscle damage. No puncture wounds. No toxins or drugs in the blood screen. No sign of trauma to the body."

Flynn pointed to discolorations on the skull, one arm and thigh.

Cecilia's eyes followed where his hand indicated. "Bruising consistent with the fall to the pavement."

She shook her head. "I reviewed the two other autopsy reports, too. Went over them about ten times. Three incidences of sudden cardiac arrest. Forensically, the only conclusion is that they died of natural causes. Coincidences that defy probability. If I didn't know better, I'd say coincidences, all the same."

"But you know better?" Flynn probed.

"I can't prove it, but lightning didn't strike these three guys dead. My gut tells me they were poisoned, but science doesn't tell me how. I have to release his body to his next of kin. I have no grounds to hold it." She frowned, shrugged her shoulders. "It's gonna nag the daylights out of me."

"Thanks, Cecilia. Let's hope there isn't another coincidental dead body," Flynn said.

"Amen to that."

Chapter 10

Kay tightened the belt on her fluffy white bathrobe, and then continued clearing some dishes off the wooden picnic-style kitchen table.

The twins still lingered over breakfast.

"Momma, don't forget to ask Aunt Matty how Flowers is doing, okay?"

How could Kay forget about her sister-in-law's rescued dog when Amanda and Peggy talked about her endlessly? "I won't, Peggy, and please don't talk with food in your mouth."

"Tell her we can help her take care of Flowers. We are very careful and gentle with her," Amanda babbled, a chocolate-milk mustache rimming her lips.

Kay smiled and plucked a tissue from her bathrobe pocket. She wiped the chocolate off Amanda's face and kissed the top of her head, inhaling the sweet shampoo scent of her hair.

"I'm absolutely sure Aunt Matty knows you both want to help her with Flowers," Kay remarked, "but I promise I will remind her this morning when I see her."

Matty, a veterinarian and a sucker for any animal, had "adopted" another badly abused Boston terrier. The newest addition to Matty and Brian's household, much to Peggy and Amanda's delight, happened to be pregnant. The girls wanted their own dog to love and spoil—a fact they emphasized to Kay at every opportunity. Matty had promised the twins that with Kay's permission they'd have first pick of the litter, but only if they went to school every day.

God bless Matty. Her twin daughters jumped out of bed each morning eager for the school day to begin, and the school nurse hadn't called Kay recently, either. *So, I'll be taking care of a puppy soon, too. God help me.*

Resigned but content, Kay leaned against the sink, leisurely sipping coffee and thoroughly enjoying the start to the day-after-Thanksgiving holiday in her sunny kitchen.

"Come on, squirts. Hurry up, or we'll miss all the good sales," Mary hollered from the door leading to the garage.

"They're on their way, honey," Kay called.

Lumpy down jackets zipped, snow boots tugged on, hugs and kisses dispensed, the girls trundled out of the kitchen.

Kay followed them down the hall. When she reached the garage, she encountered Mary, her golden hair tied in a loose bun at the back of her neck, standing behind the open driver's door of her car.

Kay tightened the belt on her robe as a frigid blast of air chilled her. "Are you sure you want to do this today?" she asked, shivering. "It's called Black Friday for a reason."

"Amy and I do this every year, Mom. We usually don't even buy anything, but it's fun to be out in the crowds. I promise we'll take good care of the squirts." She opened the back door of the car, and the twins climbed inside.

Kay hurried to the back of the car and clasped Mary's hand.

Mary's eyes widened as she gazed at the bills Kay had deposited in her palm. "*Wow*, Mom, thanks. This is a lot of money."

"Treat Amy to a nice lunch and buy yourselves something nice."

Stuffing the money into the pocket of her skinny jeans, Mary beamed. "Thanks again. You're the best mom in the world." Her soft lips brushed Kay's cheek. "Say hi to the fam for me."

She strapped her sisters' seat belts, jumped into the driver's seat, gave a quick wave, and reversed the car out of the garage. Kay stood there shivering and waving until the overhead device triggered, the motor grinding as the garage door closed.

Back in the kitchen, Kay finished loading the dishwasher, poured a fresh cup of coffee, and then rinsed and dried the carafe. Her mug in one hand, she yanked on the stainless steel door handle of her industrial-sized refrigerator. *Best mom in the world. No better way to start the day.* Smiling, she took ten pounds of butter out of the fridge, placed the packages on the center island, and opened the pantry door. She arranged flour, sugars, spices, peanut butter and chocolate chips on the counter next to the butter.

The last two Christmases, Kay couldn't handle baking Mike's favorite Christmas dessert. Everyone had obviously missed her homemade cookies because the store-bought replacements went uneaten. They *were* pretty tasteless. This morning her sisters-in-law and her mother would join her to kick off the holiday season with a new *family* cookie-baking tradition.

Kay checked the wall clock. *Nine o'clock. There's still time for a good workout before they all show up.* Kay plugged in the extra-large coffeepot she had readied before she made breakfast, took a couple tongue-scalding swigs of coffee, and dumped the rest in the sink. After she put her mug in the dishwasher, she unlocked the back door, in case the women arrived early, and rushed upstairs to her bedroom.

Shedding her nightgown, she tossed it in a

hamper and dressed in tight black shorts and a short black top. She accessed her private gym through her bedroom closet. The gym used to be Mike's closet.

Kay had needed to train devotedly in order to pass the demanding physical test required to return to the force; her brother Danny had emphasized the necessity, acting as her mentor. Danny had realized that she couldn't spare hours every day away from her family. With her permission to eliminate Mike's closet space, Danny had hired a contractor to install a door in the wall that had connected the his-and-her closets. Then Mike's closet had been transformed into a gym that Danny outfitted with a treadmill and a rack of free weights. Kay had added an elliptical machine, a recumbent bike, and a stair climber. She loved the gym for simplifying her life as she had achieved her goal of reinstatement on the force. The workouts themselves were anything but lovable.

Music streaming through her headphones for necessary distraction, she executed reps with the free weights until her arms burned and perspiration glistened on her skin. Sweating freely, she hopped on the treadmill with enough allotted time for an hour more torture. Her feet pounded the conveyor belt, blending with the rock-beat percussion through her earphones.

****

Flynn drove through the morning city traffic, the Santa file on the seat next to him. He should head to the office first, but his promise to update Kay after his meeting with the ME provided a handy excuse to see her again.

Unfortunately, he had nothing new to report on the so-called case. Nothing substantiated homicide. *What about a healthy forty-year-old man who drops dead from a heart attack? What do the loved ones say? "He was never sick a day in his life." Sad, but it happens all the time. What do we have here? Three elderly men, outside in the bitter cold, fatally stricken by sudden heart attacks. Weird that volunteerism for the same organization connects them. Uncanny that the deaths occurred in such close proximity to each other.*

Instinctively he agreed with Mrs. Heller and the ME. *But. Case closed. Disappointing. I like working with her. Maybe she'll suggest some investigative tactic that eludes me. I've got nothing.*

Steering around the circular drive, Flynn parked in front of Kay's house. He hadn't called first, so he hoped he'd find her home. Grabbing the file, he left the car, jumped the three steps up to the top of the stoop and rang the front doorbell. No answer. He knocked on the door three times, yielding no response. Bounding down the stairs, he strolled the arching driveway to the garage and peered in the window. Kay's car was there. *Hmm.*

Skirting the perimeter of the house, he tested the doorknob on the back door, surprised when the door opened. *What? Is she crazy, leaving the door unlocked?*

Standing in the middle of her kitchen he called, "Kay! It's Flynn! Your door was open."

A garbled noise resounded.

"Kay?" Flynn shouted as he strode through the hallway leading to the front entry.

The unidentified noise, like someone strangling, sounded again above him. Ascending the stairs slowly, he heard screams. Heart pounding in his chest, he bounded up the rest of the stairs two at a time, freeing his gun from his shoulder holster.

I'm coming, Kay. I'm here. The screaming continued, louder as he apparently neared its source. He burst through a bedroom door, following the shrieking and now the sounds of bludgeoning, toward a walk-in closet. Entering the closet, he crouched at the side of a doorframe. Inhaling a quick steadying breath, Flynn shoved the door open and rushed forward, gun drawn. *Kay in the crosshairs? Her feet pounding the shit out of a treadmill belt, eyes closed and screaming like a banshee?*

Her eyelids raised and she clamped her mouth shut. The shrieking ceased, but the sound of "bludgeoning" continued with her thudding footfalls. In an instant her eyes widened, apparently stunned, and she lost her footing. Flying backward, she crashed into a wall, the continuous motion of the belt pummeling her legs. Flynn leaped forward and pulled the emergency cord on the treadmill, stopping the belt.

"What the *hell* is wrong with you?" Kay rubbed her shoulder.

"I heard screams and a commotion that sounded like a fight with blunt objects." Squelching a spontaneous laugh was nearly impossible, but he managed restraint as he offered his hand to help her up. The black spiky hair was plastered around her pale face. Her shirt stuck to her body. *God. Even dripping with sweat she looks beautiful.*

"Are you out of your mind, coming into my house with your gun drawn?" She slapped his hand away and stood up using the wall for support. "What if my children were in here?"

"I'm sorry. I really thought you were in trouble. Scared the shit out of me." He tugged her into his arms, desperate to hold her and lower his blood pressure. Passion replaced fright, and his blood pressure stayed right where it was.

"I was singing." She squirmed against his chest.

"Huh?" He held her by the shoulders and looked into her twinkling eyes.

"I wasn't screaming. I was singing along with my music." She placed her hands on her hips, earphones dangling around her shoulders, all piss and vinegar. Then she howled with laughter, tears streaming down her face.

Caught up in the hilarity, Flynn burst out laughing. "You call that singing?" he asked, incredulous. "Sounded like someone was being tortured."

"Ha," she retorted. "You're not the first person to have that opinion."

"I'll bet."

She narrowed her eyes, which prompted a chuckle from Flynn.

"When Mike Jr. was a toddler," Kay paused as she pulled the terry hand towel off the bar of the treadmill and wiped her arms and face, "We took him to Christmas Eve Mass. I do love Christmas carols so much. My favorite is "Holy Night." Anyway, I guess I got a little carried away. Perhaps I was singing a little too loud when I felt a tug on my jacket. I looked down and my little boy requested angelically, 'Mama no sing. Ears hurts.'

"Thank God, only my brother Jimmy and my husband witnessed the request. If my other brothers had been there, I would never have lived it down. I bought Jimmy off with home-cooked meals." She laughed but Flynn could see the pain in her eyes when she talked about her dead brother.

He wrapped his arms around her, then lowered his head and kissed her. She tasted like coffee and peppermint—sweet, addictive candy. He ended the kiss and gazed into her crystal blue eyes. "You know," he confided. "I have fantasized often the last few nights of having you hot and sweaty in my arms. This is not exactly what I had in mind." He kissed the tip of her nose.

"What exactly did you have in mind?"

He snickered at the Cheshire grin on her face.

"A little of this." His skimmed his hand over her breast, cupped it.

"And a little of this." Now he trailed his hand downward over her damp top, her flat stomach and massaged between her legs. She gasped.

"And this." He lifted her off the floor, his hands on her bottom, and covered her lips with his.

Her legs locked around his hips and Flynn immersed in the pleasure of deepening the kiss, lost, enthralled.

"Yoohoo! Kay where *are* you?" squawked an amplified female voice.

"Bloody hell, what is that?" Flynn roared.

Kay slid down his body, the friction an electrifying sensation. She rushed to the intercom on the wall by the door and depressed a button.

"I'm in the gym, Mom. I'll be right down," she mouthed near the speaker.

Releasing the button, she faced Flynn and quipped, "Crap, it's my mother."

Kay glanced at the wall clock. "With a gun pointed at me, I forgot they were coming."

"Understandable," he teased. "They?"

"My sisters-in-law and my mother are here to start holiday baking. You blanked it right out of my head, *Captain*." Eyes wide, she gave him a bratty sneer.

"What are we going to do?" Kay paced in front of the treadmill.

"What's the big deal?" *Besides the fact that I'm visibly aroused.*

"Big deal? I just told you, my mother is here with my sisters. We're *upstairs*. In my bedroom?" She wagged a finger in the direction of his crotch, confirming that his arousal was indeed, visible. "What are they going to think?"

"They are going to think we are two colleagues going over a case together," Flynn suggested.

"Okay, good, yeah, that will work." She paced back and forth.

"One problem," Flynn said, "in addition to working in your bedroom." He grinned.

"What?" she spit out, a frown line creasing her forehead.

"When I heard you," he paused to make italic motions in the air with his fingers, "Singing, I dropped the file I brought to review with you, somewhere in the kitchen."

Kay halted in front of him, desperation in her eyes.

"Hey, Kay." Another woman blared through the speaker. "Molly is about to touch the flour. I think you better get down here fast."

"I'll be right down," Kay responded, working the intercom.

"We have to go," she declared. "I'll think of something on the way down."

Flynn followed Kay into her closet, gratified that all the pacing and hollering had effectively "calmed" him down. He filed out through her bedroom and down the stairs behind her, pleasantly distracted by her cute rear end and shapely legs in spandex shorts.

"I left the file in the kitchen, Captain," Kay commented loudly as she walked down the hallway to the kitchen. Molly, Bobbie and Mrs. Sullivan sat at the table drinking coffee.

"Morning, ladies," Flynn greeted them as Kay searched the kitchen for the file.

"Hi, Mom, Mol, Bobbie, Matty. Did any of you see a manila folder? I left it here for Flynn to pick up. I reviewed it this morning, made some notes in it, and Flynn needs it back."

"I picked a file up off the floor, honey," Kay's mother leveled amused eyes at her daughter over the rim of her coffee mug. "I put it on your desk in the office."

"Thanks, Mom. The office is this way, Flynn,"

Kay flicked her eyes toward the inner hallway. "I'll grab the file and show you to the front door." Kay's flushed cheeks belied her matter-of-fact demeanor.

"Bye, ladies." Flynn grinned at the beaming women and then ambled down the hallway next to Kay.

"Are you coming to the party on Saturday, Flynn?" Bobbie sang out.

"What party?" He stopped and faced the kitchen.

"The Sullivan Annual Secret Santa party."

"Uh." Flynn shook his head. "I wasn't invited."

"Consider yourself invited now. Right, Kay?" Bobbie's smile looked innocent, but Flynn suspected she was having wicked fun.

"Definitely. You should come," Kay reiterated.

Having fun, Flynn stepped back into the kitchen and inquired, "When and where?"

"Saturday night, seven-thirty at Paddy's Pub," Molly chimed in.

"Do I need to bring anything?"

"We call it Secret Santa, but honestly, the men buy us something nice and we get them joke gifts." Bobbie laughed. "So all you have to bring is something special for Kay."

"Thanks, I'll be there. See you Saturday night." He met Kay in the hallway and walked with her into the office.

Kay lifted the file off her desk and handed it to him. "You don't have to bring a gift for me."

"I'd like to. I'll call you later and we can go over the notes you made this morning."

"Real funny." Her face lit with her smile as she unbolted the front door and opened it.

"So you're okay with me coming to the family Christmas party?"

"Yes." The warmth in her deep blue eyes, the wide smile on her delectable lips, stirred him.

Tempted to taste her lips again, he kissed her

cheek discreetly since her family remained feet away and the door gaped open. He started down the steps and hesitated, turning around.

"By the way. Don't leave your back door open like you did this morning," he advised her.

"I just left it open so my family could get in."

"If you want them to have access to your home, give them keys."

"Yes, sir."

Holding her face in his hands, he kissed her, nosy neighbors be damned. "I don't want anything to happen to my girl. I'll call later. Save a few cookies for me."

He hopped down to the paved walk, rounded his car in the driveway, opened the door and sat behind the wheel. Kay waved as he pulled out into the street and then shut the door.

Flynn braked and stared at the closed door, already missing his girl. *Mama, no sing. Ears hurts.* He slapped the steering wheel dissolving into laughter. The absurdity of defending Kay with a deadly weapon against her own vocalizing tickled him, and he belly laughed at the memory.

Composed a couple minutes later, he accelerated and drove down her street. A devilish impulse to regale her brothers with the story occurred to him. *She bought off Jimmy with home-cooked meals.* Kay made Flynn hungry, too. For her.

Chapter 11

"Mom, are you dressed? Can I come in?" Mary's muted voice reached Kay as she finished dressing in her closet.

"Come on in, honey," Kay sang out. "I'm almost ready."

Kay walked to the adjoining bathroom and scrutinized her face in the vanity mirror as she fastened a pearl stud in her earlobe.

"You're wearing *that*?" Mary leaned against the door jam.

"What's wrong with my outfit?" Kay tugged on the tailored white blouse, self-conscious at Mary's disapproval.

"There's nothing wrong with it, if you're going to work. But seriously, Mom, you're going to a party. Where's that dress you bought at the outlets?"

Kay shrugged her shoulders.

"You know the one I mean. The green one with the pretty ruffle," Mary insisted.

"That's too dressy and it's too tight," Kay responded.

She had fallen in love with the green velvet dress, trimmed at the bottom with a red-white-and-green plaid ruffle, when Mary and she had shopped the premium outlet stores two years ago. Only that one style in all the racks, and miraculously it was tagged her usual size six. The designer label and whopping discount had Kay snagging the find without trying it on.

At home, Kay had eagerly slipped it on to model for Mike, and it was so tight he couldn't zip it up in back for her. Mike had held her that night and assured her that her figure was perfect, concluding the dress was labeled wrong. Kay missed his tenderness so much.

"Here it is." Mary carried the dress, encased in a plastic bag, to Kay's bed and laid it down. "At least try it on, Mom."

Kay unbuttoned her blouse, tossed it on the bed and slid the dress over her head.

"Mom, you have to take off your pants."

"Why bother? It's not going to fit anyway." To prove her point, Kay stuffed each arm into the armholes, prepared to pull the thing back off.

"Look at that." Mary zipped the dress up in one easy motion. "It fits even with your pants on. Perfect."

Kay posed in front of the floor-length mirror on the bathroom door while Mary ducked back into the closet. Foraging under the dress hem, Kay unzipped her slacks and let them fall to her ankles. Stepping out of her pants, she kicked them aside. *It feels great. I love it.*

Mary emerged from the closet swinging a pair of black velvet pumps on her fingers. "These shoes would be perfect with the dress."

Kay squinted at the four-inch heels.

"Just try them on, and if they don't make your legs look killer, then I'll regroup," Mary declared.

Kay slid each foot into a shoe. *You're right again, Mary. Perfect.* Kay twirled in front of the mirror. "I feel like Cinderella."

"You look hot," Mary contended.

Flattered and delighted, Kay smiled at Mary, who now scrutinized her face.

"Let's do something with your makeup," Mary said, her tone commanding.

Kay sat down at her vanity table obediently and let Mary rifle through her makeup drawer. Any cosmetics that Kay deemed too showy could always be washed off. This time alone with her daughter was too precious to resist.

"Is Captain Dowd going to the party?" Mary asked off-handedly, as she opened an eye shadow case.

Mary loaded a brush with powdery shadow and speared it toward Kay's eyes.

Kay lowered her eyelids. "Yes, he is. Your Aunt Bobbie invited him." She kept her eyes closed as the brush skimmed over her lids; handy that she could hide her bubbling anticipation over being with Flynn at the party, and truthfully could attribute his invitation to Bobbie.

"Wait 'til he sees you. You will knock him dead," Mary predicted.

Kay's eyes sprung open. "I work with Captain Dowd. I'm sure he won't notice what a subordinate officer wears off duty."

"Oh come on, Mom. He likes you."

Kay squirmed, not ready to discuss a relationship with a man other than Mike with their daughter. "What gives you that impression?"

"Because he looked at you with those goofy eyes at Thanksgiving."

"Goofy eyes?" Kay laughed. "What are goofy eyes?"

"You know, it's like when Dennis MacDonald looks at Amy at school. He looks all moony and can't tear his eyes away from her. You know, kind of goofy." Mary giggled.

Kay's eyes met Mary's in the mirror and she laughed, too, encouraged by her daughter's good-natured expression. "Are you okay with Captain Dowd giving your mother goofy eyes?"

No response. Kay gazed at Mary's reflection as her daughter played with a silver heart on the chain around her neck with downcast eyes. Mike had given it to her on her sixteenth birthday.

Mary raised her eyes, Mike's eyes, and smiled sadly at Kay. "I'm fine with you finding someone who will make you happy, Mom. I want you to be happy again," she professed, her expression sincere, tears glistening. "I will never forget Daddy, and I know you won't either. But you have to go on living."

Tears welled, and Kay stood and gathered Mary in her arms. She hugged her tight and whispered, "You are wise beyond your years, honey."

Back in her seat under Mary's hand, Kay asked, her tone casual, "Anyone at school giving you goofy eyes?"

A hint of heightened color in her cheeks, Mary replied, "No one that I want to talk about right now. What do you think?" Mary pointed to the mirror.

Kay focused on her own reflection. Her blue eyes, delicately lined with dove gray shadow and liner, appeared huge. Her naturally long eyelashes seemed false with the coat of mascara. Just a trace of pink blush enhanced her milky skin. "Sweetie, you're amazing. Wow, is that really *me*?"

"You look awesome, Mom." Mary patted Kay's shoulder and gave her the sweetest smile.

The doorbell rang.

"That must be Aunt Molly," Kay supposed. "She offered to drive me to the party. Uncle Danny will meet us there later. I think Aunt Molly has Amy with her to help you babysit the girls. Nana is staying at their house tonight to take care of your cousins. "

"Cool. I'll let them in."

****

Flynn shot his hand out and prevented the foil-wrapped box on the passenger seat from sliding onto the floor when he applied the brakes. The stop-and-go traffic drove him crazy. The dashboard clock mocked him. *I should have left earlier.* He hated to be late but had no alternative with the holiday shopper traffic in the city.

Frustration eased when he snagged a parking space across the street from Paddy's Pub. Grabbing the package, he exited the car, deposited money in the parking machine, and set the ticket on display beneath the windshield. Dodging moving cars, he crossed the street to the pub. Flynn shoved the heavy front door open. Laughter echoed and the sweet, yeasty smell of beer made him thirsty. There were no vacant seats at the sprawling mahogany bar, occupants hunched over mugs of beer, cocktails and plates of fish and chips. Reminiscent of homey establishments near Galway Bay. Flynn instantly liked the place.

The Sullivans, waving and grinning at him in greeting, sat around an oval table in the corner of the bar area.

"Yay, Flynn's here," Bobbie said as Flynn approached the table.

"Hey, Flynn! It's about time," Pat remarked.

Warmed by their hearty welcome, as if he were their long-lost brother, Flynn took the open seat next to Kay.

"Sorry I'm late. Traffic was a bitch." He stowed the package on the floor under the table and on the upward motion straightening in his seat, he kissed Kay lightly on the cheek.

"You didn't miss anything. Danny just got here, too." Kay smiled.

"You look amazing," Flynn whispered in her ear, her jasmine scent filling his senses. "Want to leave?"

His lips grazed her ear. A tiny shiver ran through her.

Kay swiveled her neck in Flynn's direction, head bent downward as she confided softly, "Tempting. What I most want..." She drew away, laughed gleefully, and asserted to the table at large, "I can't wait for our order to arrive. I'm starving."

Pat filled a mug from the pitcher of beer in the middle of the table and slid it in front of Flynn.

"Thanks." Flynn swigged a quarter mug of beer. "That hit the spot. It's been a long week."

"Anything new on the Santa case?' Pat relaxed in his seat as he stretched his arm behind Charlie's chair next to Flynn.

"Nothing new." Mimicking the gesture seemed a good idea to Flynn, and he possessively rested his arm on the back of Kay's chair. "Very frustrating, but it might be time to close the case and move on."

"No shop talk," Bobbie decreed.

"Sorry, Sis," Pat said.

"Has Mikey heard anything from John Jay College yet?" Danny propped his elbows on the table across from Kay, his chin on his knuckles. "I sent the recommendation letter."

Kay's eyes filled with tears. Flynn reached for her hand under the table and clasped it, confused.

She dabbed the corners of her eyes with a linen napkin. Still clutching it in her hand, she met Danny's eyes and replied, "No, he hasn't heard anything yet. I know it's selfish, but I hope they turn him down."

"That's highly unlikely, Sis." Danny shook his head. "His grades are the highest in his class at the community college. You know, Kay, the only reason he even went to College of DuPage was because he was afraid to leave you after Mike's death."

Flynn squeezed Kay's hand at her crestfallen expression. "I know," she admitted. "But why does he have to go to New York? He could find a college closer to home."

"John Jay is the best, Kay. He deserves the best," Joe added.

"Of course he does," Kay said with a melancholy half smile. "I just can't stand the thought of his leaving."

"My dad lives in the city, and ever since Emma was born, he's a changed man. He'll be there for Mikey if he needs anything." Bobbie smiled.

"He'll have tons of family to rely on. My parents and sister live just over the bridge in Jersey," Charlie said. "He'll be fine, Kay."

"My sisters are spread out all over the east coast," Flynn commented. "I'm sure they would help Mike if he needs anything."

Kay gazed at Flynn. "Your sisters don't even know us."

"I hope we can change that soon." *I want them to meet my lady.* "That is, if you'd like to..."

Kay patted his hand. "Of course I'd like to meet your family."

Flynn glanced around the table and read enthusiastic acceptance in the women's smiles, the guarded expressions on Kay's brothers' faces.

The waitress brought a platter of spicy, scented nachos. *Can't get those in a pub in Ireland.* Flynn's stomach growled.

Kay chuckled. "Skip lunch again?"

"I ate a huge lunch," Flynn said, "hours ago." He piled tortilla chips covered with beans and melted cheese onto his plate and topped it all off with a generous helping of sour cream.

Forks clicked against porcelain as the group devoured the food.

The waitress returned to clear the first course away.

"Okay, present time!" Bobbie reached under the table and placed a small package in front of Joe as he withdrew an envelope from his jacket pocket. Kay's other brothers handed envelopes to their sweethearts and accepted small, wrapped presents in return.

Flynn retrieved his oversized box in comparison,

and set it in front of Kay. "I guess I didn't get that memo about envelopes only from the men."

"Don't apologize for such a beautiful package," Kay stated, her expression delighted. She bent at the waist and fished around under her chair, producing a box wrapped in red paper, tied with green ribbon, for Flynn.

Squeals of delight from Bobbie drew Flynn's attention.

Bobbie jumped up waving a piece of paper overhead. "You are the *best*." She plopped in Joe's lap, threw her arms around his neck and kissed him, a thorough lip lock. Up for air, she announced to the group, "A cleaning lady for a month! I love you." She plastered another deep kiss on Joe's obviously grateful lips.

"Did that note say a month? I meant six months." Joe chuckled at Bobbie's wide-eyed expression.

Kiss number three landed and lingered before she stood and resumed sitting at the table, grinning from ear to ear. "Bet I get it up to a year after tonight," she vowed suggestively.

Joe swatted her butt playfully with his napkin and then shrugged his shoulders. "A year it is."

In unison with the rest of the clan, Flynn unwrapped his gift, revealing a cherrywood box nestled in tissue paper.

"It's a cigarette box," Kay explained. She smiled and added, "I hope you have to return it."

"Ha. I'll try to store only my watch in it or something. Thank you, Kay." He made to open the wooden box, but she placed her hand atop his. "Maybe you should wait to look inside." Her eyes danced with merriment.

Flynn lifted the lid an inch and peeked inside. His booming laughter had the family and other pub patrons craning their necks in his direction. Kay blushed.

"What's in the box, Flynn?" Pat's fingers halted over the half-untied ribbon on a gift bag.

Flynn snapped the lid shut, but one of the condoms popped out and slid into his lap. Kay burst into giggles.

"Nothing, Pat," Flynn lied, observing Charlie's eyes track the condom slipping between his legs.

Charlie winked at Kay. "Open your gift, love," she directed Pat, diverting his attention back to the gift bag on the table in front of him.

Relieved, Flynn addressed Kay in a whisper, "Go ahead and open your gift. Two great minds think alike."

Kay questioned him with her eyes, then tore the foil paper off the package and removed the box top. A soft, dark green, Kate Spade purse nestled in red and green tissue paper. "Oh, this is beautiful. You shouldn't have. It's much too extravagant," she exclaimed.

"My sister suggested it," Flynn admitted.

Kay unzipped the purse, detected the supply of condoms inside, and then quickly zipped it closed. "*Really?* Your sister helped you with this gift?" Her cobalt blue eyes danced.

"The purse part."

The noisy group, caught up in their gift exchanges, paid no attention to either Kay or Flynn.

Kay set the purse in her lap, a pensive expression on her face.

His stomach dropped. His voice low, he inquired, "Are you mad? I didn't mean to offend you."

"Mad? Of course not. I just wish the purse were bigger."

Kay's unfettered laughter contagious, Flynn laughed hard enough to bring tears and attract the family's curiosity, judging from their questioning expressions.

Thankfully, the waitress brought their dinners and an end to the Secret Santa portion of the evening.

****

Cocooned in the warmth of Flynn's car, Kay eased her head back against the soft black leather.

"I had a wonderful time with your family. They're a great bunch of people." Flynn's eyes crinkled with his smile. He glanced in the rearview mirror, changed lanes, and exited the highway toward Kay's neighborhood.

His hand curled around hers on the console. "Your hand is freezing." He disengaged, twisted the heater knob to high, and then enveloped her hand in his again.

"Bobbie is so funny. Before this night is over, I'm sure she will have a cleaning lady for life," Flynn predicted.

"She has Joe wrapped around her little finger. It hasn't been easy for them. They went through such a tough time but came out stronger and more in love," Kay related. "I had a wonderful time tonight, too. I *really* liked your present." She laughed.

"What's so funny? Besides a satchel of condoms..." Flynn grinned.

"I've never actually owned a condom before. I like it. Very empowering. I'm looking forward to using my gift soon."

"I'd like to help you put it to the best use," Flynn teased.

He braked the car in Kay's driveway in front of the house and unbuckled his seatbelt. Leaning over the console his fingers cupped her face. His lips neared, closer, until they met her lips. Her eyes closed involuntarily, and Kay melted into the kiss, straining against the seatbelt taut against her chest. Her hand fumbled and released the belt to lean closer to Flynn.

Kay jerked away from him when the porch light flashed on and brightness flooded the car. "Uh-oh. Someone knows I'm home. I better go."

Flynn released a low moan, but he opened his car door. Rounding the front bumper, he opened her door and extended his hand.

Kay clasped his hand, and he helped her out onto the driveway.

"I want you soon, Kay," he murmured, his green eyes boring into hers. He pecked a kiss on her cheek, so at odds with the thrilling, sheer desire emanating from his eyes.

Kay climbed the stoop trancelike, unlocked the door, waved to Flynn standing in the driveway, and then closed the door behind her.

"Nice, Mom. Real nice." Her son sat above her on the landing at the top of the stairs, contemplating Kay with a disgusted expression on his face.

"Mikey, what are you doing up?"

His bare foot tapped against hardwood. "It's *Mike,* Mom."

The disrespectful attitude and his angry tone set Kay's nerves on edge. "Are you mad at me for something?"

"I *saw* you."

"What?"

"I saw you acting like a slut in the car."

Kay dropped the box containing Flynn's gift on the floor, bounded up the stairs and slapped his face.

Eyes wide with shock, he touched his cheek. A red blotch raised on his pale freckled skin.

Too furious to feel guilty, Kay confronted him, "How dare you talk to me that way?"

He narrowed his eyes, defiant. "Good thing I was the one who saw you. What if one of the twins saw you acting like that?"

"Acting like what? I kissed a man good night. I didn't do anything wrong, Mike."

Tears glistened in his eyes. "Yes, you did! What would..." His voice cracked.

And so did Kay's heart as she finished his sentence, "Dad say? He would say that he wants me to be happy."

"I don't think so," Mike spit out. Standing, he presented his back to Kay, flinging a white envelope over his shoulder.

Kay's eyes followed the letter as it flew downstairs and landed on the floor at the bottom.

Facing forward, Mike had stalked halfway down the hall. "Michael Joseph, you get back here," she demanded.

He ignored her and disappeared inside his bedroom. Kay slapped her hand on the banister, a stinging whack, when his door slammed.

Exhausted, she plodded down the stairs, picked up the white envelope and inspected it. Addressed to him, it was already open, so she withdrew the official-looking letter inside and read:

Welcome to John Jay College! We are so excited that you have chosen to become a member of our community. To ensure your success, we would like to invite you to join us for Orientation on Tuesday January 25th from 10:00 AM to 2:30 PM at the College's North Hall, located at 445 West 59th Street.

Tears streamed. *It's official. After the holidays, I'll lose Mikey.*

Crushed, Kay gathered up her gift from Flynn in her arms and switched off the lights. Mounting the stairs, Kay's chest ached with self-knowledge. She was a woman with needs, but she was a mother first.

Goodbye, Flynn.

Chapter 12

Flynn heaved the last of the boxes into the Dumpster and plowed through the accumulating snow toward the stationhouse. His bent head provided slight defense against the stinging wind hurling ice against his face. He forced the door open, battling the wind's resistance, and tramped inside. Half frozen in his shirtsleeves, yet exhilarated from the consecutive polar plunges he'd made during this morning, he anticipated the start of the workday with relish.

The duty roster promised more Kay on the job today. "More Kay" had Flynn anticipating every day with relish.

Brushing snow off each shoulder, he ruffled his hair, triggering a spray of frozen confetti on the steps that he mounted in twos. Back at his desk, his office now an oasis of uncluttered organization, Flynn rocked in his chair and watched the swirling blizzard against the windowpane. He had gladly worked twelve-hour days through the rest of the Thanksgiving weekend and into midweek, handling the considerable backlog of cases within the district that required his expertise, just so he could sit that morning, enjoying the peaceful respite while contemplating a snowfall, and free his schedule to co-work the Santa case with Kay. *Although after the meeting with the St. Nick Society today, we'll probably round-file the case.*

"Dowd! Lynch! In my office, *now!*" Pat roared.

Flynn lurched in his seat, frowning. *Hmm.* More curious than obedient, Flynn rose and strode out of his office.

Kay stood at her desk and stared at Flynn wide-eyed as he advanced toward her. He smiled, his heart somersaulting at the mere sight of her. Clad in tailored cream slacks tucked into brown boots and a pale beige fisherman's sweater, she was as picture-perfect as the Christmas snow swirling outside. She bustled forward and met Flynn outside Pat's office door.

"Good morning," Flynn greeted her, his hands itching for contact with her creamy skin.

Rolling her eyes, she quipped, "Maybe not so good after *he's* done with us?"

Flynn chuckled as they entered the captain's office shoulder-to-shoulder.

"Good," Pat barked. Standing, knuckles on his desk, he seemed ready to pounce. "I want an explanation..."

"Did Mikey call you?" Kay blurted. Stiff, her arms at her sides, her hands clutched the material of her slacks. Tension seemed to waft off her in waves. "He gave me the cold shoulder," she rambled. "Wouldn't let me explain..."

"What the *hell* are you talking about, Kay?" Pat interjected. He grabbed two thin newspapers off his desk in each hand and jerked his arms forward. "Have you seen this?" His tone implied they damn well should have.

Flynn furrowed his brows and collected the newspapers, handing one to Kay. He glanced at the masthead, *Township Talk*. Staring into Pat's eyes, he responded, "No, I haven't seen this. Why?"

"Page two," Pat said, his speech clipped. "You can't miss it."

Pages rustled as Flynn and Kay opened the newspapers. "Santa Slayer's Victims Mount," Flynn read. The subtitle explained Pat's earlier roar. *Due To Police Negligence.*

"Bonnie Heller contacted the reporter," Pat said while Flynn and Kay continued to scan the article.

"*Township Talk?*" Flynn raised his eyes from the newsprint and regarded Pat. "Never heard of it."

"Local," Pat said. "*But.* All the major networks have contacted me for comment. They're running with this in local broadcasts *this evening.*"

"What did you tell them?" Kay asked.

"That we're actively pursuing all avenues to investigate the recent deaths to *determine* if foul play is involved. All evidence to date supports death by natural causes."

"Right," Flynn stated. "Can you request a retraction?"

"Of course I will," Pat glared at Flynn. "But this shit's out there, and the public perception that there's a serial killer at large will take hold. Explain to me how you plan to reverse this."

Kay tossed the newspaper on Pat's desk. "We have an appointment with the manager of the St. Nicholas Society to End Hunger," she glanced at her watch, "in an hour. I spoke to Ceci Martin this morning, and she's rerunning labs on Cy Bailey's autopsy. Frankly, she's obsessed with this case, Pat. Um, Captain," Kay rephrased as Pat's face contorted with disapproval. She sighed and then added, "*If* these men were murdered, we *will* pursue and apprehend their killer."

"All right," Pat grunted, exasperated. "Flynn, can you work up a profile on the theoretical perp?"

"Christ," Flynn muttered. "Off the top of my head? Perhaps a psychotic who didn't get that rocking horse under the tree when he was three, or possibly a religious fanatic on a crusade to purge the secular out of Christmas, or how about anyone who hates fat men in beards? Give me a break, Pat. We have no method, much less motive."

"I know," Pat conceded. "Mother of God, *Santa*

Clauses?" Suddenly Pat's surly expression transformed and he snorted a laugh. "Can you see the news feed? *Santa Claus is dead. CPD captain to blame.*" He shook his head, laughing. "Go put this to rest once and for all."

"Yes, sir," Kay responded.

"We're on it, Pat," Flynn assured.

****

Kay parked in a loading zone and trudged through drifts to the sidewalk. Peering down the block, she located Flynn through the haze of snowfall as he rounded the corner from where he had parked. She shivered as flakes rained down on her, waiting for Flynn to jog awkwardly over to where she stood in snow so deep it almost rimmed her knee boots.

The petite woman in jeans and a red sweatshirt bearing the St. Nicholas Society logo greeted Flynn and Kay at the door of the storefront establishment. "Hi, I'm Sandra Walker, Managing Director of St. Nick's Society. Welcome."

"Ms. Walker, this is Detective Kay Lynch, and I'm Captain Flynn Dowd." Flynn and Kay presented department IDs for her inspection.

The pretty blonde waved off their credentials, stating, "I trust you. Please let me show you around a moment. Then we can sit in my office so you can tell me what you need from me. Sound good?"

"Yes, thank you," Kay said.

Flynn's nearness as they trailed behind Sandra Walker both comforted and disturbed Kay. The past five days had been a blur of misery and indecision. Mikey's intractably sullen disposition since her purportedly slutty display offended and infuriated her. *So unfair. So disrespectful.* She had raised her son better, she had thought—had always viewed him as non-judgmental, equitable and, at the very least, courteous. He obviously viewed her relationship with

Flynn as inappropriate and a terrible affront to Mike's memory. *Could he be right?*

Mike had been ripped away from life in a split second, leaving her without sure knowledge of his ideas about "carrying on" as his widow. The thought of tarnishing Mike's memory and an irreconcilable disagreement with her son made her sick with foreboding. The thought of banning Flynn from her life forever made her heartsick.

Kay loved Mikey unconditionally. *I always will.* Flynn at her side spurred dizzying yearning. Sandra Walker pointed out the locker room area and the costume closet housing racks of red velvet "Santa gear" trimmed in white fur. Sandra's pleasant chatter reduced to a jumbled hum as a persistent mantra in Kay's mind drowned out the woman's monologue. *I love Flynn, too.*

Shown to the director's office, her beverage offer declined, Kay and Flynn took seats in front of Sandra's desk. Smiling widely, Sandra addressed Flynn, "I made copies of the Heller, Walton and Bailey personnel files for you, Captain Dowd." She handed folders across her desk to Flynn.

"Very efficient," Flynn commented after bestowing on Sandra a full-dimpled smile. "Thank you."

"Yes, thank you," Kay repeated. "You do understand that we don't have a subpoena for these records as yet? You're under no legal obligation to provide them."

"Oh, I want to help any way I can." Sandra smiled back at Flynn. "These men were the *nicest* people. We're very close here." Head tilted coquettishly, her hazel eyes gleamed as she conversed with Flynn as if Kay weren't in the room. "I also have Ginny Walton's personnel file for you...Gary's wife. She volunteers as Mrs. Santa during our annual fund drive." Another file exchanged between Sandra and Flynn.

"That's interesting. Let me see that last file," Kay said. "Was Mrs. Walton with her husband on duty when he died?"

Sandra referred to a sheaf of papers. "No."

Scratch an eyewitness to question. While Kay shuffled pages, Sandra expounded further to Flynn. "We do thorough background checks of all our volunteers before we accept their applications, Captain. We also conduct training before we assign a post to any volunteer."

Blah, blah, Captain. Is the woman fixated on the rank or the man? "Really? What sort of training?" Kay asked, raising her eyes from the file.

"Hospitality, role play, script review and finally, quizzes on proper procedures," Sandra responded gazing into Flynn's eyes.

A shimmer of jealousy bit Kay. She glanced at Flynn. His passive, not too attentive expression appeased her. "Ms. Walker?" Kay said to draw her attention.

Sandra shifted her gaze to Kay's face. The toothy smile Sandra had repeatedly lavished on Flynn beamed Kay's way. *Okay. The lady's just plain nice to everybody. Get a grip, Kay.* Kay rephrased the sarcastic question in her mind about possible quiz questions for Santa Claus. *Bell ringing procedures?*

Instead, she inquired, "What procedures are associated with volunteering for your organization?"

"We have procedures in place for the volunteers' protection," Sandra explained. "They all carry cell phones with pre-programmed speed dials for the Society's general number, police stations nearest their posts, and 911 dispatch. Unfortunately, donation pots have been robbed in the past." Sandra wagged her head. "There have been incidents of taunting, kicking, accosting in general, some with injuries. We train volunteers in conflict resolution, body language, and non-combative communication techniques to prevent escalation of conflict, too. Since we implemented these emergency procedures, we've virtually eliminated these sorts of problems."

Kay nodded. "Good." She straightened in her chair. "Did the deceased volunteers in question activate the emergency procedure before collapse?"

Sandra shook her head. "No. That's why I didn't call the police myself. It doesn't appear that they were threatened or attacked, otherwise they would have used their phones."

"Can you think of any reason someone would do harm to these three particular men?" Flynn asked.

"Absolutely not. They really were sweeties," Sandra asserted. "You would have loved them."

The sentiment touched Kay and fueled her ambition to ferret out motive. "Sandra, could someone be targeting the Society itself?"

Sandra's face fell as if Kay had reprimanded her.

"Please don't take offense," Kay persuaded. "I'm impressed with your organization...and you. I'm just trying to examine any possible motive."

"I understand. And I've given this a lot of thought. *Maybe* there's something to consider. I arrange for all charitable solicitation permits for the various posts during our Christmas fund drive. I've lost these three locations this year since I have no one to fill the vacancies. The permits were snapped up by another non-profit organization called The Bell Ringers. It's pretty much a national group, but St. Nick's widespread presence in Chicago precluded their entering our area. I hesitate to make accusations." Sandra fiddled with her watch, her eyes downcast.

The eyes Sandra raised and fixed on Kay swam with dismay. "The thought that any charity could possibly...I pray it's not true that three good men are dead because they worked for me."

Kay reached across the desk and patted Sandra's hand. "You've been very helpful, Sandra. May we take these files with us?"

"Of course. Let me know if I can provide anything else."

Kay stood up, glancing at Flynn.

Taking the cue, Flynn rose from his chair; three files bundled in the crook of his arm. Shaking Sandra's hand, he said, "Thank you for your cooperation. We'll be in touch."

The storm had dumped an inch of snow on Kay's windshield during the brief meeting.

"Get in and put the heat and defrosters on full blast," Flynn said. "I'll help you clean it off in a minute. I have something for you in my car." He bounded down the block.

Kay sat behind the wheel, encased in igloo-white, the defroster fan making a racket. She flipped the wipers arm down a notch. Nothing but a motor's groan and useless shimmy of the windshield wipers resulted.

A glove swept the driver's window and Flynn waved a hello. "Pop the trunk?" came his muted voice.

Kay complied, opened her door, snowbrush in hand, and joined Flynn at the back of the car. "Your painting?" She studied the canvas Flynn laid flat in the trunk. "Oh, it's beautiful."

Flynn rested a hand on the upraised trunk door. "It's yours. *Destiny II* is the title." His soulful, emerald eyes held hers. "It was yours when I painted it. You're my destiny, Kay."

"Oh, God," Kay uttered as she stared at the painting. *I want you so much, Flynn.* "I can't accept it." She wagged her head. "I just..." she gasped on a sob.

Head swimming, she bent her head, couldn't

bear to say the next, "We can't take this any further."

She jumped at the loud thud as he slammed the trunk down. "Kay, look at me," Flynn demanded.

Raising her head, body quaking, she met his eyes, registered the anguish or anger in his tight-lipped expression. "Let's talk in the car," he said.

In the driver's seat, Kay turned off the deafening defroster, steepled her gloved hands and jutted them in between her knees for warmth.

Flynn slid in next to her and shut the passenger door with force. "Are you dumping me?"

"I..." she sniffled. "Mikey saw me kiss you the night of the Secret Santa party," Kay related. "He called me a slut."

"Hmm," Flynn grunted. Slouched in his seat, he stared straight ahead. "I'm so sorry," he said, his tone gentle. "It's understandable."

"*What?* You *agree* with that?" Kay protested.

"No." He rested a hand on her knee, had to feel it knocking. "I understand that he's angry and lashed out at you. He sees me as a threat. He'd see any man you're interested in that way. I'm sure he didn't mean to hurt you."

"It's unforgivable. But he leaves me no choice."

"And you choose to dump me," Flynn stated flatly.

"I can't lose my son, Flynn." The surreal whiteness blanketing the car isolated Kay, as if she were adrift in nothingness. Hollow, empty, the prospect of losing either Mikey or Flynn seemed unthinkable.

Kay ventured a glance at Flynn, stunned at the tear that rolled down his cheek. *Dear God, this man lost his son. How could I be so insensitive?* She clasped his hand, raised it, and held it over her heart. "Flynn, darling, please forgive me."

He faced her and gave her a melancholy smile.

"Forgiven, because you called me darling." Dimples bloomed with his smile. "You need to talk with Mikey. You're a young, beautiful woman. Only you can decide if you're capable of loving another man besides Mikey's father. You can't let your son govern that decision. You determine what's best for you and then help your son and daughters understand. He loves you fiercely, Kay. As he should."

What's best for me? Just holding Flynn's hand close to her heart seemed the answer. "You're very wise." She grinned. "And I like your describing me as beautiful."

His stare penetrating, Flynn said, "I want you, Kay. I want to exhaust that stash of birth control we gave each other. But if that doesn't work for you morally, I'm okay with that. No pressure. I want you in my life. And if you want me, too, I'll help with Mikey."

I want you with all my heart. "Thank you," Kay simply replied.

"You're not dumping me?" Flynn's cocky half smile had her chuckling.

"For the moment, no."

"Good." Flynn's face neared hers, his lips hovering a breath away.

Fully understanding that she owned the decision, Kay touched his lips with hers. Closing her eyes, she deepened the kiss, open to the delicious, consuming sensations. Involuntarily her lips parted and she tasted fresh mint on his tongue, desire gathering in a knot at her core. Now the snow blanket on the car represented a hideaway to Kay, a secret, safe place that delighted rather than isolated her.

She wanted to stay there forever, hidden away from judgmental children and naysayer brothers. But she ended the kiss, bolstered by the transport to that fantastic place only Flynn inspired.

"Is your offer to help me clean off the car still good?" Kay asked.

"Uh-huh," he responded, motionless in his seat.

"Want to get going?" She rested a hand on the car handle.

"Stay inside. I'll do it." He jutted an arm into the back seat and picked up the snowbrush. "Not to mix business with…distinct pleasure, but I'll check into the Bell Ringers. Can you review the personnel files? Maybe set up interviews with the victims' families?"

"Sure."

A peck on her lips, and he jumped out of the car. In increments, the outside world came into Kay's view through the windshield, Flynn at its center.

Chapter 13

Flynn rapped his knuckles on the pane of glass before he opened Pat's office door a crack. "Got a minute, Pat?"

"Sure, Flynn. Come in." He gestured with an extended hand to sit on a chair in front of the cluttered desk.

Flynn spun the chair around and straddled it. "I've been working on the profile for the Santa Slayer."

Pat shook his head and twisted his lips in distaste.

"I hate the press moniker, too," Flynn agreed interpreting the expression on Pat's face. "I've reviewed the files, and in my opinion, there is no Santa Slayer. I want to officially close the case." Flynn smiled. "If we ever officially opened one in the first place."

"What about that rival organization the director brought up? I read Kay's report," Pat stated.

"The Bell Ringers. No red flags for any of the principals in the background checks I ran. Honestly, Pat, I can't come up with a motive." Flynn stood and ran his hand through his hair. "The Bell Ringers operate soup kitchens and homeless shelters, so they're almost direct competitors with the St. Nicholas Society as to donation use. They also derive their major funding from charitable donations during the Christmas season, but their volunteers don't wear Santa Claus costumes. The majority owner of this non-profit seems to be an upstanding member of the community: a wealthy real estate developer on the east coast.

"If I stretched it a mile, he might fit the profile of a murderer, bent on knocking out the competition to expand market penetration here, but I can't make it fit. Without post mortem evidence that the three volunteers were murdered, we have no basis to continue the investigation."

Pat's desk phone trilled. "Excuse me a sec."

Flynn leaned against the windowsill, his arms crossed, while Pat took the call.

"Sullivan. Hey, Charlie. I will. I promise." He laughed, his face lit with merriment. "I mean it this time. I'll be there in less than an hour. Love you, too." Still smiling, he hung up the phone and checked his watch. "I have a half hour to clear off this desk and get out of here, or Charlie will have my head."

"Plans for the weekend?"

"Big plans. Charlie's sister Emily and her fiancé, Jamie, are spending the week with us. Jamie's family has what they call a cabin in the Michigan woods, and we're heading up there this afternoon for the weekend. The forecast says more snow tonight. We want to get on the road before the storm hits."

"You said they call it a cabin. What do you call it?" Flynn sauntered closer to Pat's office door.

"A freaking mansion." Patrick leaned back in his chair. "The cabin has ten bathrooms and even more bedrooms. It will be perfect for the kids." He stacked the files on his desk in piles. "Charlie planned the weekend for all the nieces and nephews. Sledding, skating, and snowmen. Tell you the truth, I can't wait."

"You'll need those bedrooms and bathrooms to accommodate all the Sullivans." Flynn smiled at the memory of Thanksgiving bedlam at Pat's house.

"We'll fill up ten bedrooms with Danny's and Kay's kids."

"Kay and Danny are going with you?"

"Nope. Just the four of us with the kids." Pat's blue eyes held Flynn's. "Kay will be home alone all weekend."

Flynn read Pat's pleasant yet pointed expression as approval, but he wasn't ready to discuss Kay with her brother. Noncommittal, Flynn posed, "Anything I can do to help clear off your desk?"

"No, thanks. I have it covered. I'm out of here."

Pat rose from his seat with athletic vigor and skirted his desk.

Slapping his huge mitt on Flynn's back, he said, "Have a nice weekend."

Flynn gave him a half-smile. "I will. Good luck with the kids."

"Thanks, pal."

Flynn's spotty concentration on a final review of Cy Bailey's St. Nick personnel file was entirely due to distracting thoughts of Kay. He raised his eyes from the file and rubbed rough hands over his face. *Kay will be childfree this weekend.* He closed his eyes. *Kay is going to be naked in my bed tonight. Make it happen, Flynn.* He lifted the phone from its cradle and dialed her home number.

"Hello," she gasped, apparently out of breath.

"Hi. It's me. Did I interrupt something? You sound like you just ran a marathon."

"Sorry. I had to run to catch the call before it went to voicemail. I was out front waving goodbye to the girls and Mike."

"I just spoke to Pat and he told me he was taking the kids away for the weekend."

"Crazy, isn't he?" She giggled. "I'm probably an awful mother but, wahoo! Freedom!" Kay's laughter sounded in his ear, prompting Flynn's wide smile.

"And I'm probably an awful opportunist..." *Naked in my bed.* "My first thought when I heard his plans involved our spending the night together." He paused.

"Hmm."

Flynn tensed waiting for further comment. After a couple seconds he added, "We can start with dinner."

"Yes, I'd love that. The caller ID displayed your office number. How much longer for your shift?"

"I can leave now. I told Pat we're deep-sixing the St. Nick case."

"All right. Come on over to my house and I'll fix dinner for us," she offered.

"Why don't you come to my place? I'll cook for you." *When I hold you naked in my arms, it will be in my bed, not your dead husband's.*

"You can cook?"

"Of course I cook." *Sort of.*

"I would love to come to your place for dinner tonight. What time?"

"How does seven sound?"

"It sounds perfect. Can I bring anything? Wine, dessert?"

"I think I have everything." *As soon as I ransack the prepared foods case at Whole Foods.* "Just bring yourself."

"See you at seven," she promised.

About to disconnect, a request occurred to him, "Wait, there is something you can bring."

"What?"

"Bring your new purse." Flynn laughed as he hung up the phone.

****

I guess four o'clock on a Friday afternoon is a little late for good selections. In front of the supermarket display case, Flynn peered through the glass. The only remaining choices would hardly suffice: two deflated crab cakes, a couple slices of dried-out cheese pizza, and several bottom-of-the-bowl salads. *Not very appetizing. Chinese takeout would be better.*

Flynn speed-dialed the only number he could think of to send out an SOS.

"MDO Designs. How may I help you?" His sister's receptionist answered, and Flynn grimaced.

Miss Dorman is one scary lady. Her clipped tone reminded him of his third grade teacher, who had picked on him so much he had stuttered for years.

He followed the usual course of action dealing with the woman—exaggerated politeness. "Hello, Miss Dorman. This is Flynn Dowd. May I please speak to my sister?"

"Flynn, how are you? It has been much too long since you have been home for a visit. Your sister misses you. *When* will you be home?"

He pictured the sour disapproval on her unsmiling face. "I'm not sure, hopefully soon."

"The holidays are upon us, Flynn. Plan a trip soon."

"I will, ma'am. Is May there?" Flynn smiled. Dorman hated his using the nickname.

"*Maeve* is in a very important meeting, but I know she will take your call."

"Thank you, Miss Dorman." Flynn rested his elbows on the shopping cart.

"Hey, Flynn. Everything all right?" Maeve's lilting accent, a little New York and a lot Galway brogue, was a sound he loved.

"Hi, princess. I have a minor dilemma and thought my baby sister could help."

"Anything for you, Flynn. What do you need?"

"Can you help with my dinner party, please?"

"Dinner party? All right, who is this and what have you done with my throw-a-pizza-box-on-the-coffee-table-and-call-it-dinner brother?"

"Very funny." He paused nodding his head. "And very true." Flynn chuckled. "I invited someone to dinner. I might have exaggerated when I told her I

129

cooked."

"Might have? When was the last time you cooked?"

"I make a great omelet, I'll have you know."

"And when did you make this great omelet?"

"Fine. It's been a while. Are you going to help me or not?" he teased, knowing full well she'd never refuse him a favor.

"Don't get huffy with me. Of course I'll help you. Let me give Leo at Zabars a call. I'm thinking the honey-broiled salmon will do nicely, paired with their old-fashioned garlic mashed potatoes. They are to die for. Hmm...a lovely asparagus salad, too. I think we should start with caviar. I know, I know, a little pricey, but consider it an early Christmas gift from your adoring sister."

Wind my sister up and let her go.

Geared up to full throttle, Maeve rattled on, "We'll finish dinner off with their rugelach and brownie bites. This is making me hungry. The lucky lady will be putty in your hands. I assume that's your goal. When do you need it? Tomorrow? Sunday?"

"Seven o'clock."

"Seven o'clock, which night?"

"Tonight."

"That's not even funny, Flynn. Are you for *real*?"

"My date, who has a very healthy appetite, will arrive at my place tonight at seven." White air through the earpiece. "Maeve. Maeve, are you there?" He thought he detected breathing on the other end.

"Flynn Michael Dowd, that's only two hours from now."

"Good news, sis. I'm on Chicago time. It's three hours from now."

"I'm not laughing. Where are you?"

"I'm at the grocery store. I thought I could hit

the prepared foods case, but I'm too late."

"Go to the meat display case, grab a package of lean, trimmed boneless chicken breasts. Let me know when you have them."

Flynn pushed the cart one-handed across the store to the meat counter, cell phone to his ear. "Thanks, I..."

She cut him off, "No time for chit-chat. Do you have the chicken?"

Scanning the contents of the display case, he selected a package of chicken breasts. "Yes."

"Okay, now go to the cheese case and grab some feta cheese." Flynn reversed the cart and did as he was told.

After a foray up and down grocery aisles, Maeve's instructions guiding him, he unloaded the cart at the checkout lane.

Placing items on the conveyor belt, Flynn listened to her voice.

"I'm pretty sure you have all the ingredients," Maeve said. "Now I'll text you the recipe for my world-famous chicken Maeve Diablo."

"World-famous? Give me a break," Flynn retorted, placing the order divider behind his groceries on the belt.

"I serve an international crowd," she replied without skipping a beat. "Follow the directions, and you should have no problem. I'll keep my cell phone on in my meeting. Call if you have any problems at all when you're in the kitchen."

Gratitude swelled inside Flynn. "I can't thank you enough, princess."

"No prob. You are going to a lot of trouble for this lady. She must be someone very special."

Flynn smiled as he inched up the aisle behind the exiting customer. *She's fishing for details.*

"This lady is more than special."

"*Well.* Damn, I have to get back to my meeting.

Call me tomorrow. Let me know how *everything* turns out tonight."

"I'll call you over the weekend, and thanks again."

"I'm waiting."

"Waiting for what?"

"Your usual instructions: 'Maeve, don't tell Ma or Makayla or Maureen.'"

"You know what? You can tell them the truth. I'm having dinner tonight with a woman I can't wait for the family to meet. Thanks again, sis." Flynn snapped the cell phone shut and pocketed it.

Bags loaded in the car Flynn headed toward home. His phone signaled a text message. True to her word, Maeve had texted the recipe, preceded by, "Bring the lady to New York. What's her name?"

Flynn typed, "Soon. Kay Lynch." *The only woman besides Bree whom he'd ever wanted to introduce to his family.*

****

A light snowfall blurred Kay's view of Flynn's building through the windshield of her car. The irritating lace thong she wore bothered her and heightened the nagging out-of-her-element sensation. *What am I doing buying a new dress and uncomfortable underwear to be with a man alone? I'm not the seductress type.*

Flynn's painting had remained in her trunk. She had walked on eggshells around Mikey since they had apparently achieved a tentative peace. Without explanation, her son had simply started talking to her again. Kay didn't want to stir up a storm by unveiling Flynn's *Destiny,* as much as she loved the painting. *Is Flynn my destiny? I want him so much. Will I hurt my children if I'm selfish?* She rested her head on the steering wheel. *Get out and go to him, or turn the car around and leave.*

Her heart pounded as she slipped the chain of

the green leather purse over her shoulder and sloshed through the mounds of snow in the parking lot. *I want Flynn tonight and forever.*

Any lingering doubts vanished when he opened the door and enveloped her in his arms. Her head nestled against his chest, inhaling his clean masculine scent, his heartbeat a steady bolstering rhythm; nothing mattered but this sensation of being fully alive, a perfect fit with him. His fingers brushed beneath her chin nudging her head upward. Green eyes gleaming, he said, "*A stór.* You look beautiful tonight."

A stór...my darling. She noticed a tiny red smear near the corner of his lips as he lowered his head and kissed her. He tasted of tomatoes and wine. Their tongues teased and promised.

Flynn ended the kiss on a whisper, "Thank you." He beamed, the streak of tomato paste clownish in the crease of his smile.

"Rough day at the stove?" She reached into her coat pocket, pulled out a tissue and tenderly wiped off the smear.

Helping her out of her coat, Flynn hung it on the coat rack. His eyebrows lifted seductively as she adjusted the purse on her shoulder.

"I won't be offended if you change your mind." His eyes met hers.

Does he have doubts? Why is this so hard?

"We can still go out to dinner or order a pizza or something," Flynn said.

Kay giggled, relieved that he referred to food, not their relationship. "Nope, I won't let you off the hook. You claim you can cook. Bring it on."

She followed him to the stove. A waft of steam rose to the ceiling as he removed the lid on an oversized frying pan. Chicken, tomatoes and spices bubbled.

Kay breathed deeply, "Smells delicious." Her

stomach growled. "Sorry. I was so busy getting the kids off with Pat and Charlie that I skipped lunch."

"It won't be ready for another twenty minutes." Flynn lowered the flame under the pan as Kay's temperature spiked, fantasizing about how to spend the next twenty minutes.

He opened the fridge and hung an arm over the door. Kay fixated on his bulging bicep, itching to touch him.

"I don't have any appetizers. Would you like some Chinese leftovers to hold you over?"

"No, thanks," Kay responded.

Flynn shut the refrigerator door and faced her.

"I can wait," she said. Slipping her arms around his waist, Kay buried her hands in the back pockets of his jeans. *For food.*

****

"The Chicago police department has discontinued investigation into the recent deaths of three St. Nicholas Society to End Hunger volunteers," the man in a navy blue blazer announces into the mic. "The recent deaths of the three men were due to natural causes, specifically, sudden cardiac arrest, as certified by Chief Medical Examiner, Cecilia Martin. No evidence of foul play has been presented. We extend condolences to the families of the deceased. No further comment."

The man turns away from the microphone and a fresh-faced broadcaster's image fills the TV screen. "As you just heard, the CPD spokesperson confirmed that the police are not pursuing the alleged Santa Slayer, citing insufficient evidence of foul play in the deaths of Henry Heller, Gary Walton and Cy Bailey," she reports. "Our news crew is en route to Mrs. Bonnie Heller's home, the widow of Henry Heller. Mrs. Heller called for police to act on her suspicions that her husband and his two colleagues were murdered. Mrs. Heller's reaction will be forthcoming.

Stayed tuned to WXLS for further developments."

Well, I'll be damned. I'm that good. Had me worried there for a minute, you stupid sow. You should be thanking me. They all should. No use for those pot-bellied, sanctimonious old farts. Home free.

Almost. There's still work ahead. What's the best number? Four? Five? I like five. David picked up five stones to kill Goliath. Five is the number of God's grace, His gift to man in the Bible. I always planned to remove at least five. Now I can.

The Santa Slayer. Laughable. But might as well get into the spirit.

City sidewalks, busy sidewalks, dressed in holiday style,

In the air...the wail of sirens.

Ho, ho, ho,

Time to go.

Chapter 14

Despite her overwhelming desire to make love with Flynn, Kay's panicked heart palpitated when his hands cupped her rear end and pressed her pelvis against his, a fiery intimacy. The "new Kay" with her "new life" had experienced intimacy with only one man before. Locked in Flynn's arms, dizzy with anxiety, she would flee driven by sheer terror if she weren't so hungry for him, for this.

Attraction overtaking nervousness, Kay swept her hands upward along his back, trailing over his shirt, his muscles prominent beneath the starched cloth. Vaguely aware of how close they stood to the bubbling pot on the stove, Kay clasped her arms around his neck, steered him away from the stove and nearer to his bedroom, her inevitable destination, by a couple steps.

"I want this night to be special," he whispered. His breath fanned her ear, triggering a tingling cascade through her over-stimulated system.

In motion as one body, he waltzed her into the living room. His powerful arms around her, it was as if she floated in his embrace, unleashed from gravity and any earthly misgivings. Unsteady, she stood in the middle of the room when Flynn released her and strode over to a table to fiddle with an iPod player.

Her vision cleared and she noticed changes in the dimly lit room: a three-foot-tall artificial Christmas tree blinking multi-colored lights, the flickering hurricane candle on a crimson runner on his coffee table, a bowl of potpourri with pine cones and holly berries that smelled of pine and cinnamon.

A special night.

A flute sounded a soul-piercing Celtic melody as Flynn rejoined her in the center of the room and took her in his arms again. Piano music swelled, crystal bell tones. Phil Coulter's instrumental, "When A Child Is Born." Light-footed with Flynn as her dance partner, enraptured by the Christmas music she loved, Kay's heart soared.

"A silent wish sails the seven seas," Flynn sang, a rich tenor voice, his lips brushing the crown of Kay's head.

Kay chorused the next lyrics, "The winds of change..."

"Don't sing," Flynn begged. He chuckled, a quivering of his Adam's apple.

"Oh, all right," Kay conceded. And then she kissed his throat, snuggled her head on his shoulder.

His fingers pressed below the nape of her neck as he dragged the zipper of her dress down. Her limbs loosened like the dress hanging from her shoulders. Warm hands furrowed under the gaping cloth on her back, stroking, caressing, inciting chills.

Flynn dipped her, a rush of air in her ears. Helpless, enthralled, the roller-coaster sensations heightened as he swept her upright. A split second later, he scooped her off her feet and carried her to his bed, the walls, the furniture a blur of color on the forward journey.

Lying flat on the mattress, she quivered with longing. Her eyes closed, she trembled in anticipation as he skimmed her dress off. Her breath heaved when he dragged her bra straps down, his tongue following the path of descent along her exposed breasts. Kay wanted to scream, "Oh, God, yes!" when his mouth covered her nipple and sucked gently, a wire tightening deep at her core as she neared the breaking point.

Quaking, her hips rose and fell beneath his lips'

exploration—over her torso, her abdomen, his breath hot over her scanty underpants. He tugged off her panties and pressed his lips on the sensitive skin of her inner thighs. Her mind blanked and her body seemed to empty, an aching hollowness that only Flynn could fill.

"Oh, Flynn, *please*," Kay implored. "Make love to me."

An icy breeze fanned her inflamed skin. She opened her eyes. Flynn stood staring down at her, his eyes hooded, desire glittering in his penetrating gaze. "Green purse?" he asked.

Kay wagged her head. "No. I'm back on the pill."

His eyebrows arched. Then he ripped off his shirt, buttons scattering. He stripped off his slacks and underwear with one swift motion. The shadows afforded only brief glimpses of his naked body, but Kay thrilled at its perfection and the knowledge that this glorious man wanted her.

Flynn arched over her, covering her lips, her forehead, her neck with kisses. Crazed with desire she entwined her legs around his hips, pressing him close, closer.

"*A grhá*," Flynn said, the term like a benediction to Kay. *My love.*

He filled her, an elating completion that speared through her with rising intensity. Fused with him, her heartbeat wild, this intimate dance transported her to heights she'd never known. On gasping intakes of breath, Kay and Flynn ascended to a shattering climax.

It was as if blinding white light burst inside Kay. "My love," she exclaimed.

Limp on top of her, Flynn panted, his expanding and contracting chest a piston against her breasts. His full weight upon her pinned her on the bed—a heavy burden so satisfying that Kay wanted to sing with joy. But that would surely break this heavenly spell.

Music drifted, "Angels We Have Heard On High."

Flynn rolled, carrying her along with the motion. Securing her firmly in his arms, he squeezed her tightly and then held her on top of him, his arms loosely encircling her back. Sliding onto her side, she rested one leg over his, her palm flat on his silky chest hair. "That was *fantastic*," Kay asserted.

"Mmm," he affirmed, his expressive green eyes gleaming with warmth. "You did this for me. Thank you, Kay."

"Believe me, there was *plenty* in this for me." She grinned.

"I mean the pill."

"Oh." She bit back a laugh. "Seemed like forward thinking."

He traced his fingers along the contours of her face and touched her lips tenderly while he stared into her eyes. "I love you."

Her heart skipped a beat. "I love you, too."

Guilt dove inside Kay like an angry fist to the gut. *Oh Mike, I'm sorry.* The awful notion that her departed husband watched her in bed with another man permeated her mind. Then the irrational thought that her son's slut label for her held true fisted in her belly. Deadened by the depressing reverie, she hardly noticed Flynn's hand lightly stroking her arm, his tender kiss on the top of her head.

His chest rose and fell with each breath and his heart pulsed a steady rhythm beneath her palm. In his peaceful bedroom, blanketed with the warmth of his body, Kay's heart opened to the new possibilities Flynn's love promised. She wouldn't consider this a betrayal. *It isn't.* Instead, like his painting, which she intended to remove from the trunk of her car the minute she returned home, Kay recognized destiny.

Sleepy, she curled next to him, her nose in the crook of his neck. Sated, she inhaled his musky leather scent, suspended in a state of pure comfort, thoughts nonexistent.

Cell phones bleeped, the unmistakable call to duty.

"Shite," Flynn proclaimed.

"Shit is right."

Roused to action, they separated, shoving off the bed in opposite directions.

Flynn rummaged among the clothes on the floor and Kay ran naked to retrieve her purse in the other room. Phone to her ear, breathing hard, she choked out, "Lynch."

"Detective Lynch, I'm patching through ME Cecilia Martin."

Flynn's muted voice sounded from the bedroom, "Dowd."

Breathing heavily, Kay unfurled the afghan off the sofa and wrapped it around her like a bath towel. The dispatch connection clicked, and Kay said, "Ceci, what's going on?"

"An autopsy of another St. Nick is going on, that's what," Ceci drawled.

"You're shitting me."

"Wouldn't do that, nope. I'm going to go over this body with a fine-toothed comb. SCA, my lily-white ass," Ceci stated. "Somebody offed these guys, and I won't rest until I know how."

"Who's the victim?"

"White male, aged seventy-two, by the name of Lenny Sanders, according to the head of the St. Nicholas Society."

"Sandra Walker identified him?"

"One and the same."

"When was this?" Kay wrapped the afghan tighter under her armpits.

"Less than twenty minutes ago. The transport

just came barreling into the bay here with the body."

In motion toward the bedroom, Kay said, "I'm on my way. Flynn Dowd's with me. I'll notify him."

Ceci's laughter boomed in Kay's ear. "I just *knew* you two were lovebirds. You bring that pretty boy with you, ya hear?"

Kay's cheeks flamed as Cecilia disconnected.

Clutching the afghan against her breasts, Kay entered the bedroom. Flynn had finished dressing, except for buttoning flapping shirttails. "That was Sandra Walker," he said.

"Cecilia Martin called me," she reported, bending to scoop up her underwear. Dropping the afghan as she straightened, Kay jabbed her arms inside her bra straps, fastened it in back and pulled on her panties. "The body has already been transported to the Cook County Morgue."

"Okay. You going there?"

Kay nodded.

"I'm going to meet Sandra Walker at the Society headquarters with a forensics team. I want them to take the place apart, dust for prints, sift through the garbage—everything." Flynn put on his shoulder holster and slid a blazer off a hanger in his closet. After he donned his blazer, he approached Kay, her dress bunched up in his hands. He placed it over her head. She shrugged it on and stood in place as Flynn zipped it up in back.

"Thanks," Kay said.

Kay hurried into the front room, Flynn at her side. He opened the hall closet and took out his winter coat while Kay grabbed hers off the coat rack, threw it over her arm and opened the apartment door.

"Let me turn off the stove," Flynn said striding into the kitchen.

Racing toward the elevator, Kay reached the call button first and jabbed it with her hand. On the descent, adrenaline coursed through her. Flynn took the coat out of her hands, helped her ease into it, and then slipped his arm over her shoulder. As the elevator doors opened, he kissed her lips softly. "See you later back here?"

"Yes," she agreed, the thought of sleeping in his arms all night a welcome momentary distraction.

Outside, the frigid air stole Kay's breath. Ice crunching beneath their boots, they traversed the parking lot. Flynn's car was parked closer to the street, so Kay trudged on alone deeper into the lot to her car. Engines roared, and Kay drove out onto the street following his taillights. Flynn turned on his beacon, blue lights swirling, and cut left at the intersection as Kay sped straight through toward the morgue.

Navigating the halls of the morgue, her footsteps echoing, the fluorescent lighting cast an eerie glow. Kay peered through the window of three autopsy rooms before she spied Ceci at work inside the fourth.

"Hey, Ceci," Kay greeted her. "Making any progress?"

"Same tox panel results. Negative for alcohol, barbiturates, the usual assortment of culprits. But..." Ceci's eyes flashed with determination. "The late Mr. Sanders wore dentures. And..."

She scooted her rolling chair across the floor toward a counter, snagged a plastic specimen bag and held it aloft, dangling from her hand. "A particle was wedged between his gum line and the edge of his choppers."

Kay stepped over to her and peered at the seemingly empty bag. Examining it closer she detected a tiny speck of substance inside. "What is that? Pepper?"

"Nope. Nor is it some kind of spice or condiment. I don't know what the hell it is yet."

Kay's stomach dove as she stared lamely at the bag. "But it killed him, you think?"

"I know it." Ceci placed the bag gently on the counter. "That little bugger brought on SCA and I *will* figure out what in tarnation it is. Or I'm going to hang it up as chief ME for this city and retire in disgrace."

"Aw, Ceci. I have complete faith in you," Kay assured her.

Glancing at the corpse on the table, Kay's mind raced. "We just announced suspension of the investigation into the other three deaths."

"I know. Nice timing for the murderer, I figure."

Nodding, Kay said, "I have to notify Pat. See if he wants to broadcast this turn of events." She ran her fingers through her hair. "Flynn and I should close the St. Nick fundraising down to protect the volunteers."

"Your call, sweetie." Ceci rode her chair back over to the autopsy table. "By the way, where is your cutie pie partner?" She leered at Kay.

Squelching the impulse to relate how much she loved her "cutie pie partner," Kay responded evenly, "He's supervising a forensics team at the St. Nicholas Society's headquarters. He said he wants them to sift through the garbage, dust for prints."

"Have the team coordinate with me." Ceci pointed at Lenny Sanders' corpse and stated, "He imbibed the lethal substance. I want mugs, paper cups, plates, utensils. Anything this guy put in his mouth before he collapsed."

"Okay. Anything I can do to help you now?" she offered.

Ceci wagged her head. "Wish there was, but gluing eyes to a microscope is a solitary thing. I'll call you if I have anything for you."

"Thanks." Kay planted a kiss on Ceci's cheek. "Talk with you soon."

Kay left the building and ran to her car to escape the deep freeze outside. Clapping her hands for warmth first, she tugged off her gloves and dialed Flynn's number. "Hey," she said when he answered. "How's it going?"

"They're pretty much tearing the place apart. How about your end?"

"Ceci found a substance in the victim's mouth. She wants anything he used to eat or drink delivered to her for analysis."

"Sure thing. Where are you now?"

"In my car outside the morgue." A few flakes of snow peppered her windshield. "Should I go home?"

"No," he responded abruptly. Then he whispered, "I want you naked in my bed all night. I'll call the desk and direct them to give you a key."

Delighted at the prospect that their special night would continue, Kay agreed, "Perfect." She switched the engine on and turned up the heater. "Want me to call Pat and detail the ongoing investigation?"

"Already did. He's waiting for update from Cecilia Martin before he decides whether or not to go public."

"Flynn, I think we should advise Sandra Walker to discontinue sending volunteers to posts until we have a handle on this," Kay said.

"I thought of that, too. I have an idea about that. I'll see you at home as soon as I can."

"Okay, love," Kay replied, the endearment springing from her heart, as natural as breathing.

Chapter 15

Kay laid her hand on Flynn's bare chest and exhaled a contented sigh. He snored softly next to her. *Magical.* If someone had told Kay a year ago that her life would be filled with love again she would have considered the idea crazy. *Yet here I am. In love with Flynn.*

She circled her hand possessively along his chest. Brushing downy black hair, she thrilled at the contrast with the defined muscles beneath and willed him awake to make love to her again as he had all night.

Flynn's fingers entwined with hers, clasping her hand over his heart. "I thought I was dreaming," he said.

Resting her chin on his chest, Kay smiled.

His sea-green eyes twinkled. "You really are here."

Kay inched up, her breasts grazing his side, and tenderly kissed his lips. The comforter slipped off her shoulder. Chilly air pebbled her nipples, heightening her desire for him. Their lips locked in consuming pleasure as Flynn rolled her on top of him, filling her completely. His hands trailed up and down her back, feather light, spurring rivers of chills through her. Cupping her bottom, he penetrated deeper, her breasts pressed against his rock hard chest. Her breath caught in her throat as her hips rose and fell in increasing urgency.

A piercing climax shattered Kay's senses, set her spinning in a vortex of swirling colors beneath closed eyelids. At that precise moment, Flynn called out, "Kay!" His body tensed like steel beneath her and then relaxed, as if they both floated down to earth together.

Moments passed while Kay lay loose-limbed on top of Flynn, drained yet brimming with elation. Her name on his lips in ecstasy echoed in her mind. The wind howled, rattling the windows.

When she found the energy to speak, Kay said, "I wish we could spend the day right here and pretend there's nothing else but this." She slid onto her side, her head resting on his shoulder.

"Why can't we?" Flynn tightened his arm around her and tucked the comforter around her neck.

Toasty warm, secure, Kay wanted to remain suspended in this dreamy mindlessness. But single mother juggling necessities intervened. "I have too much to do. I have a house to clean and grocery shopping and laundry...I set up meetings this evening with wives of the St. Nick victims." *Back in the real world, where this will seem like a fantasy.*

Involuntarily her body followed her thoughts and she drew away from Flynn.

A quick flex of his arm clamped her to his side. "The chores can wait. Does your brother take your children for the weekend often?"

"This is the first time."

"That settles it. The kids are in a world of fun." His soft smile, the devilish gleam in his eyes magnetized her. "I'll help you with your errands tomorrow before the kids get home. Today is ours."

The kids are in a world of fun. Kay stared at his face. Love radiated in Flynn's eyes. The sheer wonder that this gorgeous man loved her pierced her soul. *Momma's in a world of fun today, too.* Tears stung the corners of her eyes as she kissed him.

I certainly don't need a workout today. Light spasms in her leg muscles had her extending her arms like a tightrope walker to maintain balance as she stepped into her other high heel. "I don't agree with your plan to go undercover," Kay asserted.

"Come back to bed." His back against the headboard, Flynn grinned at her, his eyes smoky with desire. *Oh, so tempting.*

"I have to go home and change before our meetings." She fought the urge to slip under the covers and just wear a dress and heels to the widows' interviews. "And don't change the subject. I'm not comfortable with you playing Santa."

"Come sit on my lap, little girl. Santa has a present for you." Flynn threw the covers off his lap.

Kay widened her eyes, laughing. "I can't believe you can still, um, deliver presents."

His eyebrows wiggled as he opened his arms.

Inching backward, Kay beamed him a smile and said, "Uh-uh. I'll meet you at Bonnie Heller's apartment at six." She cocked her head, flirtatious. "If you take a cab over there, I'll drive to the rest of the interviews, and maybe we can spend the night together again?"

"Sign me up."

Her mistake was in leaning over to kiss Flynn good-bye. More than an hour later, after a hurried second shower, Kay shut Flynn's door behind her.

The biting cold wind could not blow the smile off her face. Kay sped down the highway and reached home in record time. With fifteen minutes to change and then turn around for the reverse commute, Kay lifted Flynn's painting out of the trunk and carried it up to her gym. Expending her short reserve of time on hunting down a hammer and a picture hook, Kay hung *Destiny II* on the wall directly across from the treadmill before she shed her coat and dress in the closet and hurriedly changed clothes. *Flynn is in my life to stay.*

****

The Bluetooth connected, and Pat's voice blared

through the speakers in Kay's car, "Hey, Flynn."

"Pat, Kay's with me. We're on our way to the last of four St. Nick widow interviews. We thought we'd report in."

"You think we have a serial killer on our hands?" Pat asked.

"I'm still cloudy on why, but after the Sanders death last night, I'm convinced someone is targeting Santa," Flynn replied.

"Hi, Pat," Kay chimed in from the passenger seat as Flynn drove. "Cecilia Martin is still examining the substance she found in Sanders's mouth. She has determined it's some specimen of plant and believes it's toxic, but hasn't identified it yet. She's consulting with the Chicago Botanical Garden experts."

"I spoke with Sandra Walker last night and arranged an undercover op," Flynn related. "A messenger will deliver a handbook and a Santa suit to my office Monday, and I'll cover Sanders' post…"

"No you won't," Kay blurted.

"You object, Detective Lynch?" Pat's formality and brusque tone emphasized her lesser voice in the pecking order of decision-making here. Flynn winced, anticipating how she'd react.

"I request that you assign a uniformed officer to pose undercover, Pat," Kay said . "I think Captain Dowd would be more valuable to the department managing the op."

"No, Pat." Flynn countered. "You're short-handed, and I volunteered to work the case."

Her tension palpable, Flynn glanced at Kay when he braked at the light. She studied the roof of the car rather than meet his eyes.

Clearing the intersection, Flynn continued, "It's either this or shut the St. Nick Society down. Sandra Walker is advising her volunteers of the unknown but extremely high risk in continuing this year. I may be the only St. Nick Santa out there, we'll see."

"I agree with you, Flynn," Pat decided. "Set it up, and we'll talk Monday."

Kay remained mute.

"I'd like Detectives Lynch and Gable on this assignment," Flynn requested.

She expelled a loud breath, apparently aggravated by the whole conversation.

"I'll tell Gable at the Monday morning meeting." Pat disconnected.

Kay sat ramrod straight in her seat, her face turned toward the window as Flynn maneuvered the car through sparsely trafficked streets.

"Are you mad at me?" He reached out his hand and squeezed her knee.

"Why would I be mad at you? You completely disregard my position on this plan and flagrantly leverage your higher rank. You'll act as bait when we haven't effectively assessed the danger involved, and if I continue to confront my boss I sound like a scared little girl." She delivered her litany still facing the window. Then she stared out the windshield and shoved his hand off her leg.

"So you are mad at me." He chuckled but didn't press his luck further, and he placed his hand on the steering wheel instead of touching her again.

"Don't laugh at me." Kay stubbornly remained face forward.

"I'm not laughing at you. Why are you so against this?"

No answer.

He pulled to the curb and rammed the gearshift into park.

"What are you doing?" Kay challenged him.

"Tell me why you're upset." He undid his seatbelt. "We're not moving until you do."

Kay sagged in her seat. Facing him, she rolled her pretty blue eyes. "Fine," she said, obviously riled.

"I'm terrified I'll lose you. I *am* a scared little girl. Are you happy now? Let's go." She checked her watch. "We're going to be late for our appointment with Mrs. Walton."

"We have time." He placed his hands gently on the sides of her face and touched his lips to hers, sweet, apologetic. "I'm sorry I bulldozed you with Pat. I don't mean to frighten you. Nothing will happen to me. After all, Detective Sullivan-Lynch has my back. I trust you with my heart *and* my life, Kay."

Her eyes softened for a beat and then narrowed into a flinty glare. "If anything happens to you I am going to kill you."

"Spoken like a true mother." He laughed. We okay now?"

"I guess so," she conceded, rewarding him with a broad smile.

****

Kay knocked on the Waltons's front door and bumped back into Flynn's chest when the door swung open. Mrs. Claus in full regalia, bright red rouge circles on papery cheeks, stood beneath the doorframe. Her entire face crinkled with an expectant smile.

"Uh, Detective Lynch and Captain Dowd." Kay held her badge at eye level. "We're here to speak with Mrs. Walton."

"I'm Ginny Walton, dearie. Y'all come in," she drawled, clearing a path for them to enter her apartment.

Christmas lights twinkled everywhere. A ceiling-bumping, tinsel-covered tree stood in the corner emitting multi-colored intermittent flickers. Stuffed elves and snowmen of assorted sizes dominated the floor space and reindeer pillows lined the couch. Flynn blinked a few times to adjust to the strobe effect of flashing lights from the four corners of the living room. *Stroke-inducing.*

"I guess y'all think I'm nutty, all dressed up like this," Mrs. Walton said in a creaky voice. "I help out with Santa photos in the mall."

"Mrs. Walton, we appreciate you seeing us at such a difficult time. Our condolences on the death of your husband," Flynn said.

Rheumy, dark eyes met his. "That's mighty kind of you to say. Please call me Ginny. Why don't we go into the kitchen? I have some tea and cookies ready." She swayed a shuffling gait down a hallway leaving Kay and Flynn to follow.

"Any longer in that room and I'm afraid I'd have a seizure," Flynn whispered.

"Behave yourself." Kay muffled a laugh and elbowed Flynn in the ribs.

"Sit yourself down." Their North Pole hostess pointed to the kitchen table. Flynn and Kay sat on candy-cane-colored chairs while Mrs. Claus poured tea into holly-covered china cups. The fragrance of peppermint filled the air.

"I hope you like peppermint tea."

"This is very kind of you, Mrs. Walton, but we don't want to take up too much of your time this evening. We have a few questions." Flynn pulled a small notebook out of his jacket pocket.

"Please take off your coats and make yourselves comfortable. Try these chocolate-dipped cookies." Mrs. Walton placed a platter piled high with Christmas cookies in the center of the table.

"Please sit, Ginny." Kay patted the red-and-white-striped cushion on the chair next to her while neither she nor Flynn moved to take off their coats.

Mrs. Walton plopped down on the indicated chair with a sigh, tears welling. "I'm sorry." She dug a tissue from her apron pocket and blew her nose. "Sneaks up on me all the time."

"Don't apologize. If this is a bad time, we can

151

come back tomorrow," Kay offered.

"No, dearie. I'll live. *Somehow* I'll learn to live without Gary. What do you want to know?" She took a deep breath and trained squirrel-gray eyes on Kay.

"Ginny, did your husband have any health issues?" Kay asked gently.

"Never sick a day in his life. Every now and then my arthritis acts up and I shuffle along a bit, but not my Gary—not one ache or pain. Never complained about most anything. The man is a natural-born adventurer..." She dabbed at her eyes, shaking her head. "Lordy, I can't believe he's gone. What with him lookin' forward to the move into his dream house this summer..."

"You're moving?" Flynn asked as he took notes.

"Not without Gary. Oh, it is so unfair he was taken home to the Almighty. He finally found the perfect golf club community in Florida. The development is scheduled to open in July. So close to his dream." She blew her nose again.

"Did you know the other men who have passed on?" Kay continued the questioning.

"Oh yes. I know the Hellers and Cy Bailey. I volunteer with Gary at the Society when I'm not working at the mall. We're a close bunch. We try to get together at least once a month, off season."

"Were you working the post with your husband the night he collapsed?" Flynn asked.

"If only," Mrs. Walton sobbed. "Then at least I could have kissed him goodbye." Chin to her chest, she wept.

"Are you friendly with Susan Sanders?" Flynn inquired when Mrs. Walton raised her head.

"Can't say that I am," Mrs. Walton replied, swiping under her nose with the tissue. "Who's she?"

"She's Lenny Sanders' widow. He died suddenly last evening," Kay responded.

"Lord a'mercy. I did not know that. He's new

this year." She wagged her head, her eyes rounded. "They say death always comes in threes. Four? This is plain *awful*." Wringing gnarled hands, she stared at Flynn. "Ya know, Bonnie thinks our husbands were murdered. I thought, now, that's strong scotch. Could she be *right?*"

"Did your husband have any enemies?" Flynn asked.

"Enemies? My Gary? Lordy, no. A true gentleman is what he is."

"Did he mention anything strange happening at the Society lately?" Flynn continued.

"Not that I recall. Do you really believe someone killed my Gary?"

"I'm not sure, ma'am," Flynn said. "But I assure you, we are aggressively pursuing leads."

"You have leads?" Her eyes lit, hopeful. "What are you going to do?"

"We're working with the Society and will mount an undercover operation in the next few days," Kay related without the slightest indication of her earlier opposition.

"Really? Just like on television? Gary loves police shows. Always thought he had the answers before the police. If only he could be here for this."

"Thank you for your time, Ginny." Kay stood and extracted a business card from her purse. "If you remember anything or have any questions, call me."

"Thank you." Grasping the edge of the table, Mrs. Walton hauled herself slowly up to a standing position. "Are you sure you can't stay a little longer? I can reheat the tea."

"No, thank you, ma'am." Flynn reacted to the lost look in her eyes. "Are you all right alone here?"

Kay took Mrs. Walton's hand in hers. "Is there someone we can call for you?"

"No, there's no one to call. Do you have children, Officer?"

"Yes, I have four children."

"You are blessed. Gary never wanted children. Sometimes I regret his decision."

"Are you going to be alone for Christmas?" Kay asked, strolling hand in hand with her into the living room, Flynn at Kay's side.

"By choice," Mrs. Walton replied. "I have a sister in California who invited me to spend the holidays with her family. California? She decorates her palm tree, for God's sake. What kind of Christmas is that? I want to be here with the snow and the cold."

"Again, thank you for your time, ma'am." Flynn grasped Kay's elbow and steered her to the front door. Twisting the knob, he ushered Kay into the hallway. Before closing the door, he wished Mrs. Walton "Good night."

"I thought for a minute you were going to invite her to the Sullivan Christmas dinner," Flynn joked when they were seated in the car. He blew on one hand as he adjusted the heat vent's direction. "Christmas in sunny California sounds pretty good right now. Pine trees, palm trees, wouldn't matter to me."

"Me, either," Kay agreed. "I don't think she's thinking clearly. She'd be decorating palm trees in Florida next year if her husband hadn't died."

"Right." Flynn started the engine and let the car idle so that some warm air might blow through the heater vents.

Kay's expression was pensive as she studied Flynn's face.

"What?" he said.

"I could dress up like Mrs. Claus and work the undercover op with you," she suggested.

Flynn snorted. "Are you proposing marriage to me?"

"I'm serious," Kay responded.

He raised his eyebrows.

"About the undercover op," she reiterated.

Flynn shook his head as he shifted into drive. "No use both of us freezing our asses off. We'll see how it goes with you staking my post out from a nice warm unmarked car."

****

'Twas the week before Christmas
And all through the mall
Santa, the big cheese
Attracted them all.
The children lined up
Filled with holiday glee
Waiting their turn
On fat Santa's knee
Hurry kid or your list won't be read
Santa can't read it if Santa is dead.

Mrs. Claus checked the camera with a test digital shot of Santa as he stomped up the stairs to his red velvet throne. She chatted with the children as the long line slowly filed down the aisle cordoned with velvet rope. The doors of Fox Valley Mall had opened early for the holiday shoppers.

"Ho, ho, ho. Thanks for the coffee, Mrs. Claus." Santa waved.

"Coffee, what coffee? I didn't get you coffee," Mrs. Claus said, nearing Santa's throne.

But the screeching child a woman dragged across the parquet floor to the back of the line drowned out her voice. "I don't want to see Santa," the boy protested.

"Yes, you do, Toby. After you have a picture taken I will take you to Build-A-Bear." Apparently, the bribe of a new stuffed friend sufficed, and Toby stopped squawking.

Just drink the damn coffee. I don't have all day.
Good man. Drink it all down.
Ho, ho, ho. Time for you to go.

Chapter 16

"I want to thank you for letting me take the kids this weekend. We had a great time," Pat said, smiling, as Kay stood before his desk Monday morning. He showed his coffee cup to Kay, obviously proud of the "Favorite Uncle" imprint. "The twins picked this out for me when we stopped for gas on the way home."

"They were so excited last night they wouldn't go to bed until they filled me in on all the details. And they were predictably groggy this morning. I feel sorry for their teachers." Kay chuckled.

Pat's expression grew serious. "I know you've been worried about Mike. I made a point to spend some alone time with him. He's excited about going to John Jay. I think it's a good move for him."

Kay frowned, twisting her lips. "We're coming through a hard time, and I'm pretty sure there's another storm brewing."

"Hurricane Dowd?"

Kay nodded. "Exactly." *How do I combine my wonderful world with Flynn and my life with the children who mean the world to me? What about the rest of the family's approval?* "Are you okay with my dating Flynn?" she posed.

"The more important question is are *you* okay dating Flynn? It's not up to your children or your brothers. If it's right for you, I know you'll make it right for your family."

Kay sighed at the enormity of what lay ahead. "I invited him to dinner at the house tonight after he mans Lenny Sanders' post. I *have* to make it right with my kids, because Flynn is perfect for me." *Lord, the man even scrubbed toilets for me yesterday before the kids came home. He never looked sexier.*

"I know you will. You deserve happiness, Kay." He stood, a looming foot-plus above her, and rounded his desk. His warm embrace fortified her. Despite their spats and sibling rivalries, she needed her brothers' love.

Pat cleared his throat as he let her loose from the bear hug. "Now back to work, Detective."

"Yes, sir." Kay advanced a couple steps toward Pat's office door before she turned around and imparted, "And thank you."

****

The doorbell chimed. "I've got it, Ma!" Mary called. "It's probably Amy."

No, it's probably Flynn. Shit. Kay cast around for a paper towel to rid her hands of the sticky raw meat and egg mess.

The front door hinges squeaked faintly. "Uh, hi," Mary said. "Please come in, Captain Dowd."

"Hi, Mary," Flynn's deep voice sounded. "Please, call me Flynn."

Footsteps approached.

Economy of effort most important at that moment, Kay flung open the oven door, heat wafting over her face. She scooted the meatloaf pan onto the rack between foil-wrapped potatoes with a clatter of metal on metal and slammed the door shut. Plunging her hands into the sink, she elbowed the faucet on, rinsed her hands, and then dampened a paper towel to wipe chopped meat off the oven handle. She launched the wad of paper toward the trashcan, sunk it, and faced Flynn and Mary as they entered the kitchen.

"Smells good in here," Flynn remarked, his handsome face alight with his smile.

Standing at Flynn's side, Mary regarded Kay

quizzically. *Damn, I should have taken the time to talk to the kids first.*

"Thanks for answering the bell, sweetie. Captain Dowd is joining us for dinner."

Flynn's eyes held hers. Kay's heart skipped a beat while her stomach sank. The opposing impulses to kiss him hello or behave as if he were nothing more than a colleague in front of her children plagued her. *How do I make this work?*

She could do this. "Have a seat, Flynn," Kay offered.

He held out a bottle-shaped paper bag and gave Kay a slow smile. "I brought red wine. Want me to open it?"

The timer buzzed, and Kay reacted by grabbing a potholder and opening the lower oven door. "I'd love some wine," she replied as she removed a tray of mini-quiches. "Corkscrew is in the drawer to the right of the sink." *Just give me a straw.*

Kay plopped the tray of hors d'oeuvres atop a trivet on the center island. "Are you hungry, Mary?"

"No, I'm good." Mary backed toward the door. "I'll wait for Amy upstairs. Is it okay if I invite her to eat with us?"

"Of course," Kay said.

"Thanks, Mom." Mary left the kitchen.

"Hi," Flynn said as he placed a wine glass in her hand and then pecked a soft kiss on her lips.

Kay gulped a mouthful of wine and somehow had the willpower not to chug the stuff. A lovely warmth infused her body. "Mmm, this is good. Thank you."

"You're welcome." Flynn settled on one of the high stools fronting the center island. "Can I help with anything?"

Setting the wine glass on the counter, Kay sat on a stool across from Flynn. "You can help me eat these appetizers." She popped one in her mouth, molten cheese scalding her tongue. Dousing the fire with another sip of wine, Kay relaxed. Temporarily.

The door chime sounded. Pounding feet thundered down the stairs. The noise subsided some when Mary said, "Hey, Amy."

Thud, thud, whoosh. The twins appeared beneath the arched entry, emerging into the kitchen on "sock slides." They bumped into each other as they came to a halt. High-pitched giggles brought a smile to Kay's face. "Finish your homework?" she asked.

Clad in jeans, navy blue socks, and matching long-sleeved dark blue T-shirts with TEAM EDWARD in white block print, they also wore identical expectant grins as they caught sight of Flynn.

"Yep."

"Uh-huh."

They eyed Flynn tentatively.

"Hi, girls," Flynn said amiably as he rose from his seat.

"You remember Captain Dowd from Thanksgiving?" Kay inquired.

He approached Peggy, bending at the knees to equalize the difference in height in delivering a handshake. "You can call me Flynn. Peggy, or Amanda, is it? I can't tell you apart today."

The stair pounding resumed, and the volume of Mary and Amy's voices diminished as they climbed the steps.

"I'm Peggy."

Amanda positioned shoulder to shoulder with her twin. "I'm Amanda." Her hand jutted out in Flynn's direction. He enfolded her tiny hand in his and shook gently.

"Well," he said as he straightened to his full height. Grinning down at them, he continued, "You are identically the prettiest little girls I've ever seen."

Ooh, good strategy, Flynn, my love. They'll be smitten with you now.

As predicted, the girls' admiring baby-blue eyes never left Flynn's face as they climbed up to perch on a pair of stools. Each plucked a mini-quiche off the plate Flynn lifted from the trivet in their direction, and set to munching.

"Peggy, I saw one of your drawings in your Uncle Pat's office. You're a fine artist," Flynn remarked.

Peggy's eyes rounded, sparkling. "I signed it and everything."

"That you did." Flynn furrowed his brows. "I think it's important for an artist to use a distinctive signature on original works, don't you?" he asked, one artist to another.

Mirroring Flynn's serious expression, Peggy seemed to contemplate her position on the matter. "I do, too," she declared.

Kay's heart swelled when Peggy shifted her round-eyed gaze on her. "Momma, what does distinctive mean?"

Flynn's head lowered as he bit back a laugh.

"It means special," Kay defined.

Nodding, Peggy bit into an appetizer. Around the mouthful she said, "Right."

"Mister Flynn, do you want to see the potholder I made?" Amanda asked—not to be outdone by her sister.

"Sure..."

The back door slammed. Kay and Flynn's heads straightened simultaneously, on high alert. Mike strolled into the kitchen from the hallway leading to the garage. His open expression clouded when he caught sight of Flynn, and Kay could almost hear the door of his heart bang shut.

"Hi, honey. Flynn is staying for dinner. I'm

making your favorite, meatloaf. It's almost ready. Want some quiche to hold you over?" Kay rambled on without taking a single breath in between sentences.

"Good to see you, Mike," Flynn said rising from his seat, presumably to shake Mike's hand.

"Yeah, hi," Mike mumbled, in motion toward the sink to circumvent the island and, surely, Flynn. He turned the faucet on and washed his hands—overzealously.

Embarrassed and frustrated at her son's lack of manners, Kay's pulse escalated and her cheeks flamed. Flynn lowered to his seat, a passive expression on his face. *God knows the man has more patience than I do. Give me strength.*

While water continued to splash in the sink— *How the hell dirty can your hands be, for the love of God?*—Mary and Amy tromped down the stairs and into the kitchen. Flynn popped up from the stool again as Kay introduced him, "Hi, Amy. Do you remember meeting Flynn Dowd?"

"Hi, Amy," Flynn said.

Amy smiled sweetly, her green eyes warm with welcome—*Bless her.* "Yes. Nice to see you."

Standing next to Mary, Molly's daughter, whom Danny had adopted when they married, seemed like a negative of Kay's golden-haired child. Long black hair cinched in a messy ponytail, a snug cream sweater over jeans, Amy, like Mary, was already a man-killer. As Joe had quipped at a family gathering recently, "Those two can have *anything* they want. We have to lock them up until they're thirty."

"Hi, Amy," the twins chorused.

Amy focused on the twins and her pleasant expression darkened as she fixated on their shirts. "That is *so lame!*" she exclaimed. Wagging her finger at the twins, she ranted to Mary, "You're turning *them* against me, too? You are a spoiled *brat!*"

Spinning on her heel, Amy proceeded out of the kitchen. Mary whirled in pursuit and hollered, "Jacob has a *pig* nose!"

The twins wiggled down from their stools, grating the kitchen floorboards, whining, "I'm not a brat." They ran out of the kitchen. "Are too. *You're* a brat."

The front door slammed with sufficient force to set off tremors beneath Kay's chair.

Mike, still maddeningly presenting his back to Kay and Flynn at the sink, muttered, "You tell her, Amy. Spoiled rotten bitch is more like it."

Kay exploded, "Mikey, watch your mouth!" *I will not be baited. I will not be baited.*

Mike's body tensed, and he whirled around. "Damn it, Ma. I *hate* it when you call me that. I'm *Mike!*"

Kay rose and advanced toward her son, her finger pointed upward toward his nose. *You little shit.* "*Michael Joseph* you apologize this instant. This is no way to behave when we have company."

"*I* didn't ask *him* to be here," Mike spit out defiantly.

Kay's chest heaved and she had to clench the muscles in her right arm to prevent herself from delivering an impulsive slap to her son's belligerent face.

Floorboards scraped as Flynn apparently stood up behind her. "Calm down, son," he said. "If you want me to leave..."

Mike stared over Kay's shoulder, delivering the verbal punch, "Damn straight I want you to leave. And I'm *not* your *son!*"

Kay's reflexes were apparently off because in the next instant Mike had whizzed by her and stomped out of the kitchen. "Oh, Flynn..." Kay spun around, utterly defeated, her arms lax at her sides, and faced him. "I'm so, so sorry."

He gave her a melancholy smile as he stepped toward her and drew her into his arms. Quivering with anger and dismay, Kay barely registered the embrace, seemingly paralyzed, like a block of wood. He kissed the crown of her head and then tipped a finger under her chin, drawing her gaze to his face.

His lovely green eyes twinkled with apparent amusement.

"You think this is *funny*?"

"No." He brushed his hand softly over her cheek.

Her eyes closed a second in sheer comfort.

"I think you need to talk with the four of them." Flynn gave her a light kiss on the lips that she interpreted as farewell.

No, no, don't leave me. Kay wanted to run out the door with him.

The smell of roasting meat and baked potatoes permeated her senses. "Dinner's almost ready," she said lamely. "I'll corral them all and force them to be civil."

Flynn shook his head. "I'll be in the way. You need to be alone with them, love." He grinned. "But I'd love a meatloaf sandwich for lunch tomorrow."

Chapter 17

Kay scrubbed the makeup off her pale face with a soft washcloth. Her weary blue eyes reflected as glassy as the bathroom mirror after a restless night and a day spent buried in department paperwork. Flynn had played Santa all that day at alternating posts, backed up by Gable. She'd missed seeing him today, yet not having to face him after the dinner fiasco last night was a relief. Mike's offensive behavior continued to embarrass her.

She and the girls had eaten the overcooked meatloaf last evening in silence after Flynn had left. Mike had chosen to remain in his room, and Kay had lacked the energy to confront him. The girls' silence had carried over to this morning. Even the twins had remained subdued as they'd hurried to the school bus.

The conversation between Kay and her son before he left for school, more like a monologue, replayed in her head.

"Don't forget, Mike, tonight is family movie night."

"Huh," he grunted.

"Can you pick up the pizza? I left the money on the counter," Kay called over the banister to Mike's retreating back.

"Got it," he responded. And then the back door slammed.

That went well.

The garage door hinges squealed. *Mike is home.* Kay pulled her favorite flannel pajama top over her head and then tugged a sweatshirt on over it.

Exhausted, she would rather flop into bed and hide under the covers than face him. But she had to deal with his rude behavior to Flynn.

If my children can't accept Flynn, how will I live without him?

Ears attuned to Mike's progress upstairs, she heard his bedroom door close. She stepped out of her bedroom into the hall and advanced to Mike's room.

"Yeah," came his muffled response to Kay's rap on his door.

"It's Mom. Can I come in?"

"Sure."

Kay opened the door and entered Mikey's room, the same room he had inhabited since Mike and she had put together a toddler bed for their boy more than sixteen years ago. His man-sized bed now, made with military precision, as usual, occupied a third of the orderly room. No clutter on his computer desk, dresser top—anywhere. She had never had to nag Mikey about straightening his room.

Kay sat on the edge of the bed while he donned a CPD sweatshirt. She patted the bed next to her. Seemingly reluctant, he sat as directed, tense, as if ready for flight.

Not willing to meet Kay's eyes, he surprised her when he mumbled, "I'm sorry about last night."

She squeezed his hand, grateful she hadn't had to force the apology.

"I acted like a jerk," he concluded. His head bowed as he stared down at his huge bare feet, black hair on his toes.

Her heart constricted; her boy was now a young man. "Yes, you did," Kay agreed softly. "But I understand."

Mike raised his head, contemplating her, his bright blue eyes swimming with disbelief. "You *do*?"

"I do. Things changed for all of us when Dad died, and I don't like it one bit, either. Our lives are so different now, and, as much as I wish Dad had been here to eat our meatloaf dinner with us last night, he wasn't."

"Is that what you really wish for?" He wagged his head. "You've gone back to the force and love your job. You seem happy now." Eyes downcast again, his lips a straight line, he apparently struggled to accept that she could ever experience happiness in his father's absence.

Until she'd met Flynn, Kay hadn't believed it possible, either.

"Some mornings, honey, I wake up and lay in bed and think, 'Wow, what an awful nightmare,'" Kay said. "Then I reach my hand to your dad's side of the bed, and he isn't there. And reality sets in. It's like getting the phone call about the accident again and again."

A tear trickled down Kay's cheek. "I loved your dad. I will love him until the day I die. God willing, I will have many more years on this earth, and I need to make a new life for myself and for all of us. That's all I'm trying to do. But remember this one thing, Mike." She touched under his chin with the tip of her index finger, the skin still so soft and tender, still her firstborn baby. She gently nudged his head upward to face her. "You and your sisters are the most important people on the face of the earth to me. Nothing and no one will ever change the way I feel about you."

"Not even Flynn Dowd?" His eyes flashed and his voice cracked.

"No one." Kay opened her arms and circled his torso, hugging him tight.

Kay's eyes closed, her heart swelling. *Thank you, Mike, for our beautiful children.*

Releasing him a couple seconds later, her heart ached as he swiped tears away with the sleeve of his sweatshirt.

"Captain Dowd probably thinks I'm awful," Mike said.

"He doesn't."

With hangdog eyes he muttered, "Yeah, right."

"There are things about Flynn that you don't know. He has his own sorrows to deal with."

Mike's eyes narrowed as he focused intently on her face.

Kay continued, "Flynn understands first hand how a phone call can change your life forever—how hard it is to heal after unbearable loss. His wife and son were killed instantly in a car accident."

Mike shook his head. "A drunk driver too?"

"No, but similar. A car thief eluding the police during a chase plowed into his family's car. Flynn got the call at the roadblock set up to catch the criminal." Kay closed her eyes and shook her head. "Two more senseless deaths."

Rolling his eyes, Mike declared, "I could kick myself now for the way I acted."

"Don't beat yourself up for something you didn't know, but now maybe you will be able to cut Flynn a break."

"I'll apologize the next time he comes to dinner."

"If there is a next time."

"I hope there is." His wistful smile touched Kay's heart.

"Thank you for that. Speaking of dinner, I don't know about you, but I'm starving."

"I'm always hungry." He chuckled. "That's why I bought three pizzas, two orders of breadsticks and a large salad with your money." Mike grinned.

"Good thinking. Let's go eat."

****

Her little family sat on the floor around the oversized coffee table set with paper plates and paper napkins. Giggles and laughter filled the homey family room. A fire crackled in the fireplace, casting an orange glow on their faces.

"What movie did you pick, Amanda?" Kay asked as she wiped a smear of tomato sauce off Peggy's chin.

"I let Mary have my turn."

"I thought you wanted to watch the doggy movie again," Kay remarked.

"I did. But Mary has a special movie she made with Mikey."

Kay checked Mike's face, pleased when she noted his pleasant expression. She patted Mike's shoulder, proud that he never corrected Amanda or Peggy when they used his childish nickname. *If only I could be a little more consistent in calling him Mike.*

Mary unfolded her long legs, encased in flannel pajama bottoms, from under the coffee table. Striding toward the seventy-two-inch flat-screen TV, she grabbed the remote control. "I made this DVD for Grandma and Grandpa for Christmas. It isn't long. There'll probably be time to watch *101 Dalmatians*, too, Amanda."

"Yay!" Amanda and Peggy cheered together.

"When did you find the time to make a DVD?" Kay helped herself to another slice of deep-dish pizza and leaned back against the soft black leather couch, happy to be cocooned in her home with her children.

"I worked on it this weekend with Uncle Pat and Aunt Charlie's sister," Mary informed Kay.

"You mean Aunt Emily," Peggy added. "She asked us to call her Aunt Emily. Is that okay, Momma?"

"Of course it's okay," Kay responded. "You can never have too many people in your family."

"Do we call Mr. Dowd Uncle Flynn then?" Peggy's innocent eyes implored her. "He's our family, too, right?"

"Um..." Kay fumbled. "I think he would be happy to be included in our family. If you're comfortable calling him Uncle Flynn, I think he'd like that."

Kay braced herself for Mike's reaction, but he just gave a quick nod and stood to help Mary with the DVD player.

"Turn out the lights," Amanda demanded, but quickly added, "Please," at Mike's stern expression.

The room darkened except for the ambient glow from the TV screen.

Mary hit the play button and a black-and-white wedding photo of John and Jean Sullivan displayed on the screen. Unlined, smiling faces radiated youth and happiness.

"Who is that?" Amanda asked.

"It's Grandpa and Nana on their wedding day," Mary replied.

"But Nana has *black* hair," Amanda marveled. "Did she change it like you did, Momma?"

"No, honey. Nana's hair turned white as she got older."

Wide-eyed, Amanda stared at the screen.

A haunting melody played softly behind the slideshow of Kay's parents' wedding day, honeymoon, and life as newlyweds. The twins sat up straighter when baby pictures of Kay came next.

"Oh, Momma, you are so cute. You look just like Emma," Peggy said.

Before Kay could agree with the resemblance, something she hadn't noticed before, a montage of her brothers' baby pictures ensued. Tears welled at the sight of baby Jimmy.

"Oh, Mary. You have done such a wonderful job with this DVD." Kay patted Mary's knee.

"Thanks, Mom. I didn't do it all by myself. Mike helped, and so did Aunt Emily. She's amazing. Do you like the music?"

"I love it."

169

"It's Aunt Emily's new song. It hasn't even been released yet. She let me have a demo of it to use. Wait until you hear her sing. I looped it with the wedding pictures toward the end."

School pictures, assorted prom pictures of stiff couples in dated dress, and endless photographs of the Sullivan boys playing sports continued to play. Peggy and Amanda grabbed pillows off the couch, snuggled down on them and reclined on the floor in front of the television.

"The girls are asleep." Mary pointed to her sisters. "Is the DVD that boring, Mom?" she asked, her tone plaintive, insecure.

"Not at all, honey. Nana and Grandpa are going to love it. It's a treasure."

Emily DeMarco's lovely voice sounded, singing the song's lyrics as Kay and Mike's wedding photo appeared. "The passing time slips quickly through our hands. Wrap your arms around the love and hold it as long as you can."

"Oh, Mary. What beautiful words. And so true." Kay couldn't stem the tears that tracked her cheeks.

She smiled as Danny and Molly's, Joe and Bobbie's, and Brian and Matty's wedding images appeared. Then came a photo of Kay and Flynn, and then the whole family at Thanksgiving dinner, the finishing image. Kay stared wide-eyed at the screen. Flynn smiled into the camera as he posed next to her, his hand resting on her shoulder. The screen faded to black and the words "Merry Christmas, Nana and Grandpa" in bright white, block letters appeared.

Mary aimed the remote at the television and stopped the DVD. A news broadcast played as Kay combined the uneaten pizza into one box, her heart racing. *Flynn with me in a family keepsake.*

"I'm so impressed, honey," Kay remarked, her tone nonchalant. "When did you learn to make a

DVD?"

"In class. Next semester we're going to work with video. I can't wait."

"I took those classes last year. I couldn't stand Mr. Jumper," Mike asserted.

"Oh, he's harmless. I like him a lot," Mary contradicted him. "He lets Amy and me do whatever we want." She laughed.

"How are things between you and Amy?" Kay inquired. "She seemed pretty upset last night."

Kay stood, hefted the stack of pizza boxes, balancing them in her arms.

"She's fine." Mary collected paper plates and napkins, stepping over her sleeping sisters.

At Kay's side, toting trash toward the kitchen, Mary surmised, "She's in a major mood once a month."

"More information than I need to know," Mike quipped with a headshake as he joined them in the kitchen. He loaded silverware and glasses into the dishwasher.

"Can you make copies of the DVD? I'm sure your uncles will each want a copy once they watch it on Christmas Day. I know I would love to have one," Kay said hopefully.

"Mike, can you help me?" Mary requested.

"Sure, no problem." He closed the dishwasher. "I'll help carry the girls upstairs, Mom."

"Thanks." Kay followed Mike back into the family room. "Then, can we watch the DVD again?" Kay bent to pick Peggy up off the rug.

"I have homework to do and a big test tomorrow." Mike lifted Amanda effortlessly. When had her baby boy become such a strong young man? His muscles bulged under the sweatshirt as he carried his deeply slumbering sister out of the room.

"I'll watch it again with you," Mary offered, heading toward the television.

"Great." Kay shifted Peggy in her arms. "I'll be right down."

****

After Kay tucked the twins into bed, she returned to the family room and joined Mary on the couch, a fresh bowl of popcorn set between them. Mary triggered the DVD to play, and Kay's parents as bride and groom appeared again.

"While you were upstairs, the news came on," Mary said as they both watched the screen. "Why are they blaming the police department for the Santas that died from heart attacks? Isn't that just the way things are with elderly men?"

"That's the way it looked in the beginning." Kay dipped her hand in the bowl, grabbed a handful of popcorn and dumped the buttery-smelling helping in her lap. "But we have reason to believe that these men were murdered."

She popped a kernel in her mouth. Adorable baby pictures appeared on the screen in succession.

"Really?"

"We think someone is dosing them with something that causes the heart attacks."

"How? Who?"

"That's what we're trying to figure out. Flynn has been undercover this week."

"Oh no. Couldn't he get hurt? What if he has a heart attack? Mom you can't let him do it. Make him stop." Mary's brows knit etching worry lines on her forehead.

"Honey, he'll be fine." *From my mouth to God's ears.* "Flynn is a good cop. He can handle himself. We won't let anything happen to him. You like Flynn, don't you?"

"Yep. I do," she replied simply.

"Thank you for including his picture on your DVD."

"I wish I could take credit for it, but it was

172

Mike's idea," Mary admitted. "He added the picture of you and Flynn this afternoon before he went to pick up the pizza. He's really sorry for the way he acted last night. He even apologized to me."

The music ended as the replay of the DVD finished.

"I better get upstairs, too," Mary said. "I want to review for a quiz tomorrow."

"Thank you for a wonderful movie night." Kay stood and hugged Mary tight. "Don't stay up too late."

"I won't." Mary bounced up the stairs.

Kay upended the popcorn bowl over the trashcan, discarding unpopped kernels, and then hand-washed, dried and put the bowl in an upper kitchen cabinet. She drifted back into the family room and relaxed on the couch, only the glow of embers from the fireplace providing light.

She closed her eyes, content and hopeful—she smiled.

****

Chestnuts roasting on an open fire
Bury Santa in the ground
No one sings, not even the choir
When Christmas morning rolls around.

Five and done. The police are idiots. Good thing. But the more I think about it, why stop at five? I can't stop now. You always told me to excel at something. Beat anything you deemed half-assed right out of me. Are you proud, Father? Have I lived up to your expectations finally? Six? Now there's a number. Six Saint Nicks. Ha! Six, six, six.

Chapter 18

Flynn had somehow resisted the temptation to call Kay last night, despite his ever-increasing hunger for her. The music of her voice, the infectious trill of her laughter, had become like drugs for him. Relishing the addiction, he was as much in love with her mother's heart as each inch of her sexy little body. Flynn wanted her in his bed every night, in his life every minute.

She had to handle her children without intervention from him. Flynn respected that, but the resulting pervasive uselessness rankled him. As a cop, he was trained to overcome opposition, battle life-or-death threats, and emerge the winner. *How do I fight to win her, if her family draws battle lines?*

Even so, he envied her parenting complications. *If only I had to engineer Flynnie's acceptance of Kay.* Flynn yearned to help Kay deal with her children's reception of his relationship with their mother because more and more he wanted to make the relationship permanent. *Would I be a good stepfather...sensitive enough to co-parent with Kay as a father figure while honoring their father's memory?*

The psych degree he had earned might be useful. *Or not.* He smiled wryly as he drove his car toward the stationhouse. Trusting Kay's capacity to do the best thing for her kids implicitly, he prayed that Mike or Mary or the twins wouldn't force her to choose between motherhood and a relationship with him. He'd lose her. And if he did, he'd lose everything. Again.

As he drove into the lot adjacent to the

stationhouse, Flynn spied a figure near the entry of the building. He parked, exited the car and sped toward the front door, the subzero temperatures permeating his leather jacket. Simple inhalation stung his nostrils, and the frigid air had him squinting his eyes to slits. The ice-encrusted city landscape was cheerless, with sunless gray skies above dirty mounds of snow.

Nearing the stationhouse, the figure he had noticed earlier came into blurry view. A small person wrapped in a full-length beige down coat, a black ski cap, and a striped scarf wound around the head from above the nose to below the chin marched black boots in place a couple feet from the double doors. Nearing the building entry, Flynn identified the person as Kay by her mirth-filled sapphire eyes and her muffled voice greeting him.

"Flynn, I couldn't wait to talk to you," she sang out as she launched herself into his arms.

Her entire body quaked, surely from the wind-chilled temperature. He rubbed the sides of her padded arms. "What in the world are you doing outside?"

Kay hooked a finger on the edge of her scarf and nudged it down below her mouth. "I saw your car turn in as I was about to go through the door. I'm so happy this morning." She beamed at him, her breath a vapor fog in front of her face. "Mike apologized for his behavior. Freely given! I didn't even have to threaten his life." Her laughter rang crystal tones in the deep freeze.

Gratitude warmed Flynn and he drew her close, pressing her over-padded form against his chest. "Ah, love, I'm so glad," he whispered, his chapped lips brushing the crown of her woolen cap.

Arching her neck, she gazed into his eyes. "I think he's all right with us as a...couple. Are we a couple? I'm moving too fast. This is..."

Flynn covered her icy lips with his, sank into the kiss, spiking his temperature despite minus fifteen thermometer readings. She tasted of morning coffee and sweet seduction.

"Get a room," came a snide male voice.

Flynn drew his lips away reluctantly. Still enveloping Kay in his arms, he met the man's eyes. "Good morning, Josh."

Sergeant Josh Lucas leered at him and remarked, "Looks like it's a better morning for you than for me." He chuckled as he whipped the door open. "You guys are nuts. It's fucking cold," he tossed out before he disappeared inside the building.

"He's right." Flynn laughed. "Let's go inside," he suggested as he grasped the door handle.

He steered Kay inside within the circle of his left arm. As they mounted the stairs, she said, "Would you like to take another pass at dinner at my house? You'll be welcomed, if not with open arms, at least, I hope, with sufficient courtesy."

"Of course," Flynn replied raising the volume of his voice to compensate for the din of various timbres of ringing phones and loud conversations that registered as a roar inside the precinct. "Whenever you think the time is right. Maybe we can do something Christmassy with the kids? Catch *Welcome Yule* at Orchestra Hall, or maybe take a drive to see the lights?"

Kay smiled. "I'll put it to a vote." She clasped his hand and gave it a quick, covert squeeze. "I better hit the desk before 'Big Ben' Pat clocks me late." She rolled her eyes.

"I ran background checks on the widows and families of the St. Nick victims. I'll bring them to you in a few minutes."

"Thanks."

Flynn strode down the hall to his office, following Kay's progress toward her desk out of the corner of his eye. Somehow she managed to move gracefully stuffed into ten pounds of lumpy down winter coat. His fingers tingled as they thawed. Pins and needles pinched his face from his forehead to his chin.

Shedding his jacket inside his office, he rubbed his hands in a scrubbing motion until he had enough circulation to use them. He collected the papers that documented the background checks, tamped them in a neat stack, and reversed out of his office to deliver the documents to Kay.

"Here they are," Flynn said as he presented her with the paperwork.

"Thanks." Placing the stack of papers on her desk, she looked up at him from her seated position. "Anything jump out at you?"

"Nothing out of the ordinary. No criminal records, financial red flags—everyday people one and all. Employment records are clean. Before retirement, some victims worked blue- and some worked white-collar jobs. The wives, too. Diverse religions. Neighbors attest that the four couples are respected, popular members of the community. The only common thread, aside from the men's volunteerism for the same organization, is that all four couples are childless. I've drawn one possible conclusion from the data. The victims might be incidental to the perp's target. I think our perp kills Santa Claus, not the men who play him."

Kay grimaced, sweeping a hand through her hair, the messy effect flattering. Lately, every move she made attracted Flynn.

"Geez," she said, exasperated. "You've been undercover a full week, and that's as useless as all this." She gestured toward the paperwork.

"I'm on the Santa clock again today, starting at eleven-thirty. The lunch crush outside Macy's on State Street. Sandra Walker told me it's the prime location for her outfit. At least it's the most visible. That post hasn't been struck yet, though. Hard to figure a location pattern in the killings. I'm going to wear *two* pairs of long johns and try not to freeze my ass off."

"You do that. I've grown very fond of that ass," she whispered with a suggestive twist of her lips.

Flynn responded with a penetrating gaze, the racket around him muted in his consciousness, intimately holding her eyes as the only embrace available to him in the very public workplace.

Kay sighed, eyes glistening, a sweet smile on her lips. "Thank you," she said softly, interpreting his loving expression. She paused. Their eyes remained glued on each other, and then she said, "I'll stake out your post today and cover your frozen ass."

Flynn huffed a laugh, prompting Kay's wide smile. "Too bad I'll be on duty. I'd like to do some Christmas shopping, since I'll be so close to Macy's," she said. "I haven't even put up the Christmas tree yet."

Kay wagged her head, black hair gleaming in downcast fluorescent light. "Last year the holiday was nonexistent."

The sparkle in her lovely eyes dimmed, projecting that hollow ache of deep-seated grief that Flynn knew too well. "This year I have to get my act together," Kay declared. "Maybe muster the troops to decorate tonight. School's out this afternoon until after the new year."

"I'll help, if they're ready for Flynn the interloper." He grinned.

"I'll take you up on that."

He bent down to whisper in her ear, "We *are* a couple."

Kay nodded her head, beaming. "I'll take this paperwork with me to go over while I back you up later."

"Okay. Santa will return." Flynn left Kay's desk to spend some time catching up on his duties.

****

By eleven, Kay was bleary-eyed from reading the mundane information in the background checks.

"Lynch, line one," Lucas announced.

Kay reacted, extending her finger over the line button.

"Line two's for Lynch," a female voice hollered.

"Lynch, line five!"

What the hell?

The board lit up as Kay punched line one. "Detective Kay Lynch," she said.

In the background, a male voice called, "Cap, channel seven news, line four."

"Detective Lynch, this is Sandra Walker. I'm discontinuing further fundraising and pulling all my volunteers off their posts immediately."

Kay eyed the two other blinking lights, suspecting that the calls were connected. "Another victim?"

"Minutes after he took up his post. Terry Kingsley. I just had to notify his wife." Sandra's voice hitched on a sob. "I've waited too long to suspend collecting this year. It's my fault that Terry's dead."

Kay sympathized. "I can understand how you feel, Sandra. But we made the volunteers aware of the risks involved, and they chose to continue working. I agree with your decision to suspend activities for now." *Flynn won't back down, though. I hate it, but I can't see a better way to flush the killer out, under the circumstances.* "Captain Dowd is scheduled to man the post outside Macy's at eleven-thirty today. He'll continue with that. No other volunteers are active until further notice from me. I'll check with the officer on patrol of Terry Kingsley's location and talk to my captain about substituting more police personnel at other posts going forward. Can you open your offices to provide costumes for our officers?"

She sniffled and then replied, "Certainly. Anything you want."

"Thank you, Sandra. I'm so sorry for your loss of Terry Kingsley. Has he been removed from the scene?"

"Yes. The paramedics came," Sandra responded, her voice wavering, still apparently crying.

Blinking lights on her phone pressed Kay to conclude the conversation. "Thank you, Sandra. I'll be in touch."

Phone to her ear, she clicked line two and said, "Detective Lynch."

"Hey, Kay," Ceci Martin drawled. "I'm about to start the autopsy on one Terrance Kingsley. Since he's dressed in a Santa suit, I figured you'd want to know."

"I just heard," Kay responded. "Ceci, we've got to crack this."

"I'm on it. The paramedics on the rig brought a thermos. I already have the lab analyzing its contents. Are you on duty all day?"

"Yes. I'm leaving in about twenty minutes to back up Flynn Dowd. The St. Nicholas Society's director shut down the fundraising drive pending case closure. I'm glad she did that voluntarily. You can reach me on my cell or patch through to my unit if you have anything."

"Sure thing." The call disconnected.

One more call to go...so far. I need to speak with Flynn. A commotion sounded from the vicinity of Pat's office. She didn't have to turn around to investigate the reason for the outburst. *Here comes Pat.* Strategically Kay punched line five's button to be occupied before he reached her desk. "Detective Lynch."

"How could you *do* this? How could you let Terry *die*?" The accusatory tone overlaid the female's soft southern accent.

"Who is this, please?"

"I'm Ginny Walton, Officer. You probably already forgot me. Just like you forgot about my dead husband and all his friends."

Kay took a deep breath. "On the contrary, ma'am. I didn't recognize your voice. I assure you we are aggressively pursuing all avenues of investigation in your husband's death and the deaths of his colleagues."

"Well that's a load of bull puckey," she exclaimed. "You and that other man told me he was going undercover as a Santa volunteer. Were you *lying* just to appease me?"

"Nothing of the sort, Mrs. Walton." Kay dragged a hand through her hair and clutched at the roots near her scalp, frustrated. "All other Society volunteers are suspended for now. I intend to discuss adding police personnel to the undercover operation with my superior officer, and Captain Dowd has worked undercover, as we told you, and he will continue as planned."

"And a *fine* job he's doing," she said, her honeyed drawl dripping acid. "Who do I talk to there to report police incompetence? I think I'll call the other wives...*widows*, Officer, and we can band together to complain. I don't even believe the stupid undercover operation, as you call it, exists."

"Ma'am, my supervisor's name is Captain Patrick Sullivan. Captain Dowd reports to Superintendent O'Halloran. You may speak with our superior officers at any time regarding our professional conduct. I assure you, though, the undercover operation is proceeding. Captain Dowd will be posing as a volunteer today during the lunch rush, and he'll rotate posts around the city until the killer is apprehended. We will aggressively continue to investigate these crimes. You have my word," Kay pledged.

"Well," she enunciated the word as if it had two syllables. "I feel better now. Will you call me and let me know if you find any clues or anything? Maybe I could help?"

Pat hung over Kay, waving a hand in front of her face. "I will, ma'am. Goodbye. I already know," Kay preempted Pat's possible diatribe about the press hounding him for information about *The Santa Slayer*. "Cecilia Martin is examining the body and contents of a thermos now. Flynn and I are leaving in a few minutes to continue the undercover op. Sandra Walker closed down her fundraising drive. Who was assigned to patrol Kingsley's location? Did he or she report in yet?"

Looming over Kay's seat, Pat seemed gigantic. "Garcia radioed in when Kingsley collapsed. No one approached the victim before he keeled. The news stations are up my ass."

Kay nodded. "Can we spare some men to take up other posts with backup to bait the perp?"

"Yeah, okay. I'll get on that," he responded. "I won't release any information to the press. Can you advise Sandra Walker accordingly?"

"Sure."

Kay spied Flynn ten desks down, barely recognizable in the fat Santa suit, glossy white beard and wig, except for his sparkling green eyes. She burst out laughing as he neared her desk.

Pat's tight-lipped glare at Santa and his "helper" demonstrated that he didn't share her humor. "Just catch this sick fucker," he commanded before he spun on his heel and headed to his office.

"Ready?" Flynn asked, his eyes dancing.

"Yes." Grabbing her coat and winter gear she remarked, "We have another dead volunteer and we've closed down the St. Nick Society. Pat's working on rounding up men to work the posts with you."

"Shit," Flynn responded. "Anything to go on, with this victim?"

"Ceci Martin's working on it now." Kay shrugged into her coat and snatched the pile of background checks off her desk to review again during the stakeout. "Let's go."

Striding through the squad room at Santa's side, Kay marveled at Flynn's obvious lack of self-consciousness. She felt ridiculous.

Outside, slammed by what seemed a wall of frigid air, Kay hoped Flynn really had donned two pairs of long johns. *The weather might kill him before the perp.*

Kay halted near Flynn's car as he opened the driver's door. "Ceci will call me if she determines anything significant. I'll follow your car in one of the unmarked, and I'll park so that you're visible at the post. Work the store entrance on the corner of State and Randolph with your back to traffic. Hug the curb so I don't lose the sightline with pedestrians. If anyone offers you anything to eat or drink, cuff him."

"Yes, ma'am." Flynn grinned. "Want to sit on Santa's lap and tell him what's on your list?"

Chapter 19

"Phone call for you, Lynch!"

Kay turned in the direction of the booming male voice, its source, Tom Gable, propping open the stationhouse door.

"Who is it, Tom?" Her gloved fingers curled around Flynn's car door handle as the engine roared to life, vibrating her hand.

"Your daughter." Gable stomped his feet and rubbed his hands.

"Go back inside. I'm coming." Kay leaned into the car. "I have to take that call. I'll follow in a minute."

Flynn tugged his snowy white Santa beard down, leaned forward and covered her lips with his ice-cold mouth. His taste, his musky scent, enveloped her in delicious warmth—compelling, tempting her to climb into his lap, ignore ringing phones, and luxuriate in *more*.

"Now you can go," he murmured as their lips parted. "I'll meet you there." His sea-foam-green eyes twinkled.

Her grip tightened on the door as he tried to close it. "Don't do anything stupid," she cautioned.

"I won't. I promise."

Kay released the handle and the door swung closed. She hurried into the squad room to her desk.

Sitting on the edge of her chair, Kay removed one leather glove and lifted the phone receiver to her ear. "Mary?"

"Hi, Mom. Sorry to bother you," Mary said softly.

"Oh, sweetie, I'm sorry it took so long to get to the phone. Is everything okay?" Kay held her breath.

"We're cool. I'm officially on Christmas break as of ten minutes ago. After I pick up the squirts when they're done with school later, Amy and I are going Christmas shopping at the mall. Is it okay if we take Peggy and Amanda with us? Maybe grab dinner?"

"You must be psychic, honey," Kay replied. "I was going to call Nana after lunch to see if she could babysit for me. I might be late tonight. I'm on a case."

"Amy and I will come back to the house and watch the girls here after dinner, so don't worry about them. You know—in case you want to go...uh, out with Mr. Dowd or anything."

Kay smiled. *My sweet considerate baby.* "Honey, you are the best. I can't thank you enough."

"It's no big deal," Mary replied offhandedly.

"Thanks again. Be careful."

"Always am."

Her daughter's customary response widened Kay's smile as she hung up the phone. On her feet, Kay grabbed her glove off the desk and looped the knit scarf tighter around her throat. About to head off, her phone rang again.

"It's crazy here today." She shrugged her shoulders at Tom Gable, standing in his cubicle 'door'.

Tom rolled his eyes. "Tell me about it".

"Detective Lynch."

"Hey, Kay. It's Ceci."

"That was fast. Tell me you have something for me."

"I haven't finished the autopsy on Mr. Kingsley yet."

Kay plopped back into her desk chair, disappointed.

"*But* Murray in the lab called me a few minutes

ago," Ceci continued, an excited tone in her voice. "He has identified the substance I plucked from Mr. Sanders' dentures. It's a leaf from a genetically altered plant called Malcolmvine."

"Okay..."

"Written up in a journal of cancer studies dating back two or three decades. A controversial botanical/pharmaceutical. On one hand, it seemed to have near-miracle potential as a cancer cell proliferation inhibitor. But miniscule dosage deviations arrest the heart—SCA in less than an hour after ingestion. I have the lab running tox screens on one other Santa victim. If the powers that be over there order the other bodies exhumed for testing, want to bet we're five for five on Malcolmvine as the murder weapon?"

Kay's fingers flew across her keyboard as she cradled the phone atop her shoulder. "I'm searching this on the computer right now. Ceci, you're a magician."

"Hope it helps. You owe Murray a fistful of his favorite cigars. I'll call you when I have everything tied up in a pretty little Christmas bow." Ceci's laughter tittered in her ear before the phone clicked, and she disconnected without a good-bye.

Kay scanned the search results on her computer monitor.

Sidney Malcolm Honored by the Cancer Institute of the Americas for the cultivation of Malcolmvine.

A crackling, static sound distracted Kay. "Tom, do you hear that?" she called out in the direction of Gable's cubicle.

He emerged in the doorway facing Kay's desk, "Yeah, it's Dowd's transmitter." He reached into his coat pocket and extracted a handheld radio.

"Ho. Ho. Ho. Thank you. Help feed the hungry this Christmas." Flynn's Santa-talk emitted from the transmitter, replacing the static.

Gable brought the device close to his lips and barked, "Dowd. You copy?"

No response.

"Dowd, reply, please," Tom stated. "Not working. Maybe the cold got to his mic." Tom shook his head. "He might be able to hear transmissions. No way to know." He tossed the transmitter backward over his shoulder into his cubicle. It landed with a clatter, maybe on his desk. "I'll head out to Macy's and try to finesse switching out Flynn's headset."

"I'll take care of it. I'm leaving in a few minutes to back him up. Let me take that radio with me, too, so I can monitor him on the way."

Tom disappeared temporarily inside his cube and then lobbed the transmitter to Kay.

"Thanks." Kay placed it on her desk and refocused on the search results.

Malcolmvine Initial Clinical Trials Show Promise for Terminally Ill Men Suffering from Prostate Cancer.

Malcolmvine Clinical Trials Underway in Milwaukee.

"Hello, Mrs. Claus. What are you doing out on such a bitter cold day?" Flynn asked. "That's so kind of you. You shouldn't have. It's too cold for you to be out on the street."

A female voice responded to Flynn in the background, but the words were garbled. Kay lifted the portable radio off her desk and held it to her ear while she continued to scrutinize the information on Malcolmvine. She unbuttoned her jacket as she scanned the article.

Malcolmvine Clinical Trials Suspended after Fatal Adverse Reactions. Sidney Malcolm defended Malcolmvine to the board of inquiry. Asserting it was perfectly safe with the proper dosing protocol, the scientist cited incompetence on the part of pharmaceutical company management of clinical trials.

FDA Rejects New Drug Application for Malcolmvine...rejected five years after initial application for approval by PhytoPharmaceuticals. Sidney Malcolm, PhD Genetics, M.S. Botany, genetically engineered the plant bearing his name, Malcolmvine, for administration to advanced stage prostate cancer patients...

Kay moved the cursor to the *Google* search box and typed *Sidney Malcolm.*

Natchez, Mississippi. Sidney Malcolm Dies in Fire...conflagration spread to two buildings in the vicinity of the laboratory run by local scientist. Firefighters contained peripheral fires....survived by three children: Sidney, Jr. (Audrey), Todd (Margo) and Virginia Malcolm Walton (Gary).

"Jesus," Kay muttered. "Ginny is Sidney Malcolm's daughter."

"What's coffee without a little splash of Irish whiskey?" a woman posed through the transmitter, her voice husky, the cadence slow Dixieland.

"Smells like a little more than a splash. Thank you," Flynn said. "This'll hit the spot. Mmm. Delicious. Stay warm."

Kay grabbed the radio off her desk. Mouth to the speaker she screamed, "Oh, my God! Don't drink it, Flynn!"

Heads turned in her direction in the squad room as Tom Gable raced to her desk. "What's going on?"

Kay punched in Flynn's cell phone number on her desk console with shaky hands as beads of perspiration gathered along her hairline. No answer.

"Ah shit! Tom, come with me." Kay shoved her chair back and stood, jamming her arms into her coat sleeves.

"Where are we going?"

"Corner of State and Randolph. Ginny Walton, one of the victim's wives, is the killer. She just gave

Flynn coffee spiked with the toxin that causes sudden cardiac arrest. We have less than an hour." Kay's own heart seized as she related the facts to Tom.

She ran across the squad room, Gable at her heels and barged into Patrick's office. The door slammed against the wall with the force of her swing.

"Pat, order an APB on Virginia Walton. The file on my desk has residence details, etc. She's the Santa Slayer. She just attacked Flynn."

Kay bolted out of Pat's office. "I have to get to Flynn. I'm taking Gable with me. Send backup," she called over her shoulder.

Tom Gable had already shrugged into his jacket as he sprinted to the door, holding it open for Kay.

Bounding down the stairs, their feet echoing hollow drumbeats, Kay's pulse thundered in her ears.

"You drive, Tom," she directed, running side-by-side with Gable. "I'll keep trying to contact Flynn."

Kay slipped on a patch of ice in the lot but managed to keep her balance. Her hands trembled as she opened the passenger door of the squad car.

Sirens blaring, lights flashing, Tom raced the police cruiser through city intersections toward State Street. Traffic stalled, nearing Macy's, to nearly a complete standstill. Crowds of people swarmed the area.

"Damn Christmas tree. It's the middle of the day, for God's sake. Shouldn't these people be at work?" Gable put his hand on the horn as a group of tourists sauntered in front of the idling police car, the siren and flashing lights as ineffective with pedestrians as the gridlock of cars in front of the squad car.

"What the hell is wrong with these people? Get the hell out of the way!" Kay slammed her hand on the dashboard.

About to implode with frustration, Kay opened the passenger door. A gust of wind buffeted her face and she had to strain to prevent the door slamming shut in her face, too. A frozen mist swirled into the car. "I'll go on foot," Kay advised Gable. "Circle Flynn's location if you ever get a chance to move."

She jumped out of the car, taking a functioning two-way radio with her. Running in front of the police car, she pushed dazed Christmas shoppers out of her way. "Police. Move. Police."

The bitterly cold air ripped at her lungs like a knife in her chest as she willed her numb legs to race. She turned the corner onto State Street and zeroed in on Flynn's bright red figure in the distance. He stood at his assigned post, right arm swinging a bell.

The ringing bell, Flynn's upright posture, brought tears to Kay's eyes. Relief coursed through her. *We're in time.* Her breath ragged, she continued sprinting a weaving pattern around pedestrians.

The two-way radio bleated. She lifted it to her ear, "Lynch."

"What is your location, Detective?" Pat's voice boomed.

"I have a visual of Dowd," Kay panted. "I'm a block and a half away. Gable is circling the block."

A crowd of shoppers blocked her view of Flynn.

A shrill scream cracked the air.

Frantic, Kay elbowed through the clump of humanity. Flynn clutched at his chest and fell to the pavement.

"No!" Kay shrieked. "Officer down. I repeat, officer down." Kay yelled into the radio. "Send an ambulance. Gable, abandon the car. Come on foot."

Continuing to run, Kay's legs leaden, her mind reeled. *You stupid ass. I told you not to accept a drink from anyone.* Horns blared, brakes screeched.

Kay dodged cars, eyes darting from pedestrian to pedestrian as the possible perpetrator. She sprinted across the street, barreling toward Flynn's position. He lay sprawled on the ground, his face covered by the Santa beard.

"Step back," she ordered onlookers and then knelt next to him. "Flynn!"

Quaking, she removed the Santa hat and beard. His eyes were closed and his pale face appeared lifeless. Coal black hair matted against his head.

"Flynn! Flynn! Stay with me." Digging her frozen fingers under the fur collar, she pressed against his carotid artery, praying that she'd detect a pulse. His steady heartbeat made her weak with relief. His lips moved. She bent over him, inches from his face.

"Mrs. Claus," he whispered.

"I know. Don't talk. Save your strength. Help is on the way." *Where is that damn ambulance?*

"Closer," he rasped.

Kay leaned closer, her ear against his lips.

"Eleven o'clock," his voice held conviction, but he obviously was in shock. Or maybe the toxin was taking effect.

Panicked, Kay clicked the transmit button on her radio. "Officer down. Where is my ambulance? I need it *now*. Gable where the hell are you?"

"Kay. Listen to me,' he said, a breathy whisper. Emerald green eyes implored her. "Don't react. Walton is watching."

Kay started to lift her head, but Flynn's hand squeezed her arm. "Don't look. She's positioned at eleven o'clock over my right shoulder," his voice clear and solid.

"You're not having a heart attack?"

"No. I didn't drink the witch's brew. I set the cup down behind the collection pot for evidence."

Gable ran up the street and knelt next to Kay.

"Tom, listen to Flynn. He's not hurt," she whispered.

"Our perp is dressed as Mrs. Claus and she's behind the concrete pillar inside the entrance to the parking garage across the street. I assume she's sticking around to verify my death. Get her."

"Tom, stay with him. I have this." Kay sprang up, edged the crowd back in a wider arc, and stopped traffic on the street.

"We need to get an ambulance down Randolph," she yelled to the traffic cop at the corner. "Close off this street."

Inching her way to the other side of the street, she pointed to drivers on Randolph and diverted them in succession onto State Street. Sirens filled the air as an ambulance cleared the intersection a block away.

Kay watched Gable's and Flynn's reflections in the department store window, Flynn still prone and Gable hovering over him, continuing the ruse. As the EMT rig braked at the curb in an earsplitting blast of sound, she advanced to the mouth of the parking garage hugging close to the line of buildings.

Peering around the garage doorframe, Kay detected movement behind the pillar, a flash of red cloth. A car whizzed by, exiting the garage within inches of Kay's nose, and stopped perpendicular to the usually jammed, now empty, street. Drawing her gun as a communication tool, she pointed it toward Walton's position, staring straight into the driver's eyes. He nodded as she moved the gun in a circle as if around the front bumper.

Kay rounded the car low to the ground, slipped into the garage and flattened her back against the opposite side of the square column that concealed Ginny Walton. The car cruised away.

Clasping her gun with both hands, Kay whipped around the column's edge and yelled, "Put your hands up!"

Walton flinched and flung her arms over her head with surprising speed. "Don't shoot!" she hollered. "If I die I'll have to be with *them!* I'll do what *you* tell me."

"O...kay. Put your hands on that column," Kay demanded.

"Virginia Walton, you are under arrest for assaulting an officer." Reciting Miranda while cuffing the woman's hands behind her back, Kay observed Flynn and Gable jogging across the street in her direction.

Tom winked. "I'll take it from here, Katie boy." He addressed Walton, "Let's go, grandma."

"I *should* be a grandma but I'm *not!*" Walton screamed, a crazed expression on her garish apple-cheeked, Mrs. Claus madeup face. "That son of a bitch didn't want kids. I didn't have a choice. I *never* had a choice about *anything.* Do this, don't do that. I want, I want, I WANT, he'd bark at me. But I won in the end, didn't I? I don't have to do what Gary says anymore. Do you *hear that*, Father?" She arched her neck, addressing the sky, white eyeballs rolling in their sockets, a maniacal sight.

"I don't have to do what you say anymore, either," she ranted. "I *am* good!"

She stared at Kay. "I'm *very* good at killing, aren't I, Detective?"

Gable shook his head and tugged Walton on the arm. She resisted and faced Flynn. In an eerie singsong voice she chanted, "*No one would save him. No one would win. Not even the hot shot. The cop they call Flynn.*"

"Enough of this shit," Gable declared. "We're going to the car now." He led her away.

"Well." Black hair mussed around his chiseled cheeks, Flynn beamed at Kay, his eyes gleaming. "Smooth operation, Detective." He opened his arms.

"I was so scared," she admitted, nestling her head on his chest.

"I didn't suspect the woman until she offered me a drink," Flynn said.

"I requested an APB on her before I left the stationhouse. Ceci Martin identified the murder weapon, and I traced it back to her father. Then I heard you talking to her."

"I didn't receive confirmation through my earpiece."

"The transmitter didn't work. I felt so helpless when you accepted that drink." Her body trembled. "I was terrified I'd be too late to save you."

"Fortunately, I didn't need saving." He stroked her hair.

The radio on Kay's belt squawked, "Lynch. Report status."

Kay plucked the two-way off her belt reflexively, ready to respond to Pat, but Flynn took it out of her hand.

"Dowd here, Pat. Kay collared the Santa Slayer."

"Good to hear your voice, Flynn. Kay reported earlier that you were attacked. Are you all right?"

"Never better." A crooked grin dimpled one cheek. "Detective Lynch got here in the knick of time to catch the killer. Gable's bringing her in now."

"Good work, guys."

Flynn handed her the transmitter and then squeezed her close in a hug. Remembered terror tightened her chest. "I thought I'd lost you," she said, gazing into his emerald eyes.

"You're stuck with me. I'm not going anywhere." His lips met hers and the crowd, the snow, and the cold disappeared.

Chapter 20

Christmas Eve

The canvas in her arms, Kay navigated through the obstacle course of wrapped presents covering her living room floor, toward the fireplace. Propping Flynn's painting on the hearth, she stretched upward and unhooked the abstract print off the wall, then replaced it with *Destiny II,* careful not to edge too close to the crackling fire that heated her lower body. Standing back, she gazed at the painting flickered with firelight and the shimmering lights from the nine-foot Christmas tree in the corner of the room.

The house seemed monumentally transformed in that instant. The Lynch home had always been the epicenter of Sullivan family life, welcoming strangers and converting them into family, too. Kay the hostess baked and cooked and theme partied through the years of uproarious fun. Mike, by her side, the tender host who adored his wife, sometimes just endured the family circus because he delighted in the light in Kay's eyes when surrounded by those she loved. Until Mike's death had removed the possibility of fun within the walls of the house they had built together.

Now the Sullivan family circus was in full swing at the Lynch house again. Guffaws, chatter, high-pitched squeals, and general racket filled Kay's senses as she stood alone in her living room facing her destiny. In one of the other rooms, Flynn Dowd had joined the circus troop.

"Kay, I love you!" Joe bellowed.

He found the pumpkin bread. She stepped mincingly over presents and headed toward the direction of his voice, grinning. Entering the kitchen, she encountered Joe stuffing his face with the predicted home-baked treat. Pecking him on the cheek, she suggested, "Save room for dinner, Joe. I went all out."

Kay stirred a pot on the stove and then leaned against the kitchen counter, observing the commotion around her. Mom and Daddy sat on the bench of the huge, picnic-style kitchen table, baby Emma in Daddy's lap. Entertaining their youngest grandchildren, her twins among them, her parents beamed at the kids seated on the floor around their feet. Amy and Mary chatted with Molly and Matty, sipping drinks, Cokes for the teenagers and mulled wine for her sisters-in-law. Joe draped his arm over Bobbie's shoulder, ever possessive of his wife. Danny, Brian, and Pat—black, sandy-blonde, and redheaded, respectively—alternated non-stop eating and talking while training appreciative eyes on their women, Molly, Matty, and Charlie. Her heart swelled and tears brimmed. *I am so blessed by my family.*

"Here's the man of the hour," Pat hailed Flynn as he sauntered into the kitchen with Mikey.

"Hey, Pat," Flynn responded while he gazed only at Kay, his magnetic eyes and irresistible smile transfixing her.

He strode over to her and clasped her in a bear hug, rearing back to lift her off the ground. "No, we have a woman of the hour," Flynn declared.

Kay fixated on Mike over Flynn's shoulder, astounded at his broad smile.

Setting her down on her feet, Flynn proclaimed, "Kay saved Santa."

"Yay," chorused the kids.

Kay thought the cheer meant for her until the twins finished with, "Flynn's here!"

Not at all insulted by her daughters' reaction, instead Kay exulted at the enthusiastic reception of the man she loved. His daily presence in her little family's life the past week—helping decorate the house, working with Mike on a computer glitch, treating the twins to ice cream at the mall while Kay frenetically Christmas shopped, watching the Christmas DVD with Mary—had spurred endless longing in her to make his relationship with her children...with her...permanent. She had toyed with the idea of proposing to Flynn that night after the family left. *I might still do it, if I can talk to the kids first.*

"What's the deal with that old lady?" Bobbie inquired.

"She willingly confessed to all five," Kay arched her brows, tilting her head toward the kids. "Little ears."

Her brothers and their women clustered closer to Kay and Flynn around the center island.

"And her intention to add Flynn as number six on her list," Kay continued shuddering. "She kept ranting in Christmas carol jingles. 'Oh little town of Naples, I pray your dream house burns...' Crazy stuff like that. Flynn, do you remember that last one?"

"Yep. My personal favorite. 'Away in a manger, no babies were born,'" Flynn hunched over and whispered, "Our husbands, the shitheads, laid down all the laws. Live my way, no backtalk. Well. Fuck you, Santa Claus."

Kay snorted and then joined in the simultaneous laughter that erupted from her siblings, tears streaming down her cheeks. Hand on her chest, she caught her breath and said, "I know I shouldn't laugh at such a twisted mind. She honestly believes she was helping her friends by making them widows. She's under psychiatric observation at the lockup. I don't need to pass the bar," Kay smiled at Charlie, the defense attorney turned prosecutor, "to predict an insanity defense."

"Hey, as long as she's locked away somewhere for life, I'm happy," Pat said. Raising his glass, he said, "To Kay and Flynn. Good job."

Glasses clinked as Kay basked in the compliment a few seconds. "Thanks, Pat," she said. "Okay. Let's get this party started. Everybody!" The voices in her kitchen quieted. "How about we open our one gift before dinner?"

The fevered dash toward the living room began as if she had fired a gun at the starting line. Kay placed her hand on Flynn's arm and strolled down the hall with the parade of generations of Sullivans.

Passing through the arched entry into the living room, Flynn halted, his eyes riveted on the wall over the fireplace. "*A stór*, you couldn't have given me a better present."

"I love the painting, Flynn." She gazed into his eyes and the loving expression on his face pierced her heart with pleasure. "I love you," she mouthed.

The older kids scampered around the living room, read aloud the tags on stacked packages, and passed out presents to the intended recipients. Emma crawled the floor, ripped off a strip of wrapping paper from an unattended package, and settled down on her padded bottom to presumably eat it. Joe intercepted the paper headed toward her mouth smoothly as he scooped the baby up and covered her neck with kisses, prompting belly laughs, one of Kay's favorite sounds.

Kay had long since abandoned attempts at establishing any order in the family tradition to open one gift each on Christmas Eve, although some semblance of order reigned. Danny and Pat manned huge plastic trash bags and wadded paper flew at their collection stations from all quadrants. Settling down on the carpet, Kay sat in a lotus position, observing the pandemonium.

"Mike? Want to help me bring in a box from the car?" Flynn asked.

Passive and expressionless, Mike complied with a simple, "Yeah," as he fell into stride with Flynn and exited the room.

A few minutes later Flynn returned carrying a large box single-handed while Mike ambled companionably at his side. Plopping down on the carpet next to her, Flynn positioned the package in front of Kay. "Merry Christmas. Go ahead and open it," he said.

She leaned closer to his ear, "Publicly?"

He gave her a half-smile, apparently also remembering their Secret Santa exchange, and nodded. "It's, uh...safe for the audience."

Kay tore off the Christmas wrapping, dug at a corner of tape with her thumbnail, seized the loosened end, and ripped the tape off the box.

Opening the flaps, Kay withdrew a folded white T-shirt with black block letters spanning the front, TEAM DOWD. Mary and Amy giggled.

"Flynn?" Kay raised questioning eyes, her heart hammering in her chest.

"There's one for you, me, Peggy, Amanda, Mary and Mike," Flynn said. "If..."

He foraged beneath the shirts and produced a blue Tiffany box. Extending it toward her in the palm of his hand, he positioned himself on one knee. "Will you marry me?"

"I..." Kay stammered, lightheaded.

A cleared throat drew Kay's eyes to the sofa, where her mother and father had settled for gift opening. "Flynn asked for your hand yesterday. Your mother and I gave him our blessing."

"Oh," Kay managed, tears welling.

"He spoke with us, too," Pat declared as Joe, Danny and Brian moved to stand at Pat's side, her precious brothers united. "We said we'd be proud to have him in our family."

Tears tracked her cheeks as she met Mike's eyes across the room. "Flynn asked my permission a couple of hours ago," he said staring into her eyes. "I told him he would be the luckiest man on earth if my mother agreed to marry him." Mike strode to stand with his uncles, beaming at her.

Kay emitted a small mewling sound as her breath caught in her throat. Her baby, the little imp who had extorted money from his uncles with "bakery alerts" so her brothers had descended on her kitchen to consume everything she baked before it could cool, was gone. He had become a fine man, like his uncles and grandfather, ready to defend her decisions and love her through anything.

"Momma, I want to put on my shirt," Peggy declared.

"Me, too," echoed Amanda.

"Now that's a team we won't fight about," Mary said, elbowing Amy.

"Flynn, I'm with you on this, but I won't wear that shirt," Mike teased.

"My leg has gone to sleep," Flynn quipped.

Kay rose and extended a hand to Flynn.

He clasped her hand and stood, his eyes riveted on hers. "I love you with all my heart."

"Oh, I love you, too, Flynn." Kay tossed the shirt in her hand to Amanda. Opening her palm, her eyes trained on Flynn's, he placed the ring box in her hand.

"Yes!" Clutching the box, she threw her arms around his neck as the Sullivan family cheered and whistled.

A word about the author...

K. M. Daughters is the award-winning writing team of sisters, Pat Casiello and Kathie Clare. Their penname is dedicated to the memory of their parents: Kay and Mickey Lynch. "The Daughters" are wives, mothers, and grandmothers. Kathie lives in northern New Jersey and Pat lives in the Chicago suburbs.

In addition to their Sullivan Boys romantic suspense series, published by The Wild Rose Press, K. M. Daughters writes inspirational romance published by White Rose Publishing. "Love Heals..."

Thank you for purchasing
this Wild Rose Press publication.
For other wonderful stories of romance,
please visit our on-line bookstore at
www.thewildrosepress.com

For questions or more information,
contact us at
info@thewildrosepress.com

The Wild Rose Press
www.TheWildRosePress.com